For Nicola

Thank you
for all you have done
for Richard. Enjoy !
Alistair Lees-Smith /.

The Chest of Surprises

Alistair Lees-Smith

DEDICATION

For Sam, taking the story forward...

ACKNOWLEDGMENTS

My thanks to Emma and members of my family for their pictues and advice.

PROLOGUE

Joyce brought a copy of the Evening Standard with the headline: 'Peace in our Time' and the picture of Neville Chamberlain returning from Munich, waving a piece of paper; there might yet be hope but she had learnt not to trust politicians entirely. She walked down Argyle Street to Liberty's. The staff were very friendly and welcomed her by name. She was charmed. She took the lift with the linenfold wood panelling to reach the Oriental Department on the fourth floor where a beautifully hand-carved chest caught her eye. She immediately decided to purchase it. The manager looked a bit worried. No, her credit was good but it was the last one they had. A replacement would have to come from China which could take a while. Of course they would offer a discount in the circumstances and a cup of coffee, which was welcome. Revived and feeling a lot better, she walked out of the shop, receipt in hand.

It was nearly three years later when she received a knock on the door of her house in North Square, Highgate. To her amazement, two liveried men from Liberty's were there to deliver the large chest. She could not believe it. She had never given it a second thought. How on earth had it come all the way from China in the middle of the war. It had travelled ten thousand miles through serious fighting without a scratch. Here it was, pristine with a beautiful smell of camphor. Men had risked their lives in convoys to deliver it to Britain, possibly at the expense of much-needed food or weapons. But it had survived. It would be perfect.

"Where shall we put it, Madam?" One of them asked.

"Oh, upstairs at the bottom of the bed."

The men looked distinctly unhappy. The Chest had finally arrived.

Sixty years later, work was being done to renovate some disused buildings on the side of Hampstead Heath. The old house had seen much better days. The once elegant portico was faded and unloved. An old nameplate read 'Uvedale' beneath the cobwebs. All the rooms were empty and desolate. Builders were gutting the house completely to give it new life as flats. A worker broke through into the attic. He shone a torch to reveal, sleeping under a dustsheet, an ornate wooden chest, tucked into a large recess behind the chimney. He opened it gingerly expecting to find a body inside. This is how the detective novels start, he felt. But there were no flies, indeed no body. Certainly no gold coins. Nothing he could see of great value. It seemed to contain only a lot of old papers and photographs. Then he noticed the ribbon of the Legion d'Honneur. Unusual; I think I deserve a medal for finding this, he thought and pocketed it. More to the point if you dusted the whole thing off... perhaps this chest is more interesting than it looks. Superstitiously he closed the lid.

With a little help, he managed to get it into his van and made sure he was the last to leave. A good day's work he thought. He had nearly reached the gate when Sandy, the security guard stopped him.

"Mind if I take a look, Sir?" He asked.

He opened the rear doors.

"You do have a rather unusual toolbox." Sandy mused. "Mind if I see inside?" He opened it before the workman could reply. "Not your normal tools of the trade. I suppose you were going to take it to the local museum."

"Er, yes" the workman stumbled.

"Well, I can save you the trouble." He picked up a photograph and shook off the dust. "Once this was a great hospital. These are family papers. Please step out of the car."

A quick body search revealed the medal.

"In the Foreign Legion were we, Sir? I think I'd better have that too." And the medal was returned to the chest. "If you leave immediately, I'll not report this. I hear you are a hard worker. Otherwise it's the police. Oh, and the Border Force might be interested."

The workman looked very pale and sped off into the darkness.

With a little research, Sandy found that the nearest surviving relative was Joyce's grandson Alistair. Sandy made contact; Alistair was delighted and wanted to meet right away. They met in the Spaniards Inn in Hampstead a couple of days later. Sandy liked Alistair and knew the chest would be in the right hands. Alistair was incredibly delighted.

Sandy told him how grateful he was to the hospital for saving his leg. He remembered how well Sister Mcglashan had looked after him. He used to walk in the grounds when he had been a patient there. How elegant the house had looked then.

"I lived there for a while when I was very young. It was such a lovely place." said Alistair.

"It's a bit different now, I'm afraid," said Sandy and he explained how he had come by the hidden chest. "Uvedale would have been marvellous for children."

"Well, I suppose I was the youngest resident. I really cannot thank you enough for saving the chest," said Alistair.

"There's a story in here," said Sandy "And it's yours to tell."

1 THE BALL

Alistair had only been four when he had last lived in Uvedale but he remembered the magic chest so well. It was in his grandmother's bedroom, out of bounds of course. He used to love looking at the carved Chinese scenes, different on each side and on the arched top. He was not big enough to lift the lid, nor had he wanted to. He hesitated; this would be the start of a journey. He looked out of the window onto the rockery and a heron alighted.

Alistair opened the chest and there was a picture of Lords and Ladies at a real Edwardian Ball. He knew the story so well - his grandmother Joyce liked telling it, not least because it always irked her husband.

At the time Ambrose Woodall had been standing on the side of Berkeley Square watching the guests arrive. Large cars, even horse-drawn coaches, were pulling up; liveried servants were helping ladies to alight and escorts were guiding them up the steps. It was a bygone age. Ambrose himself represented the new rising class; his father was a poor Methodist preacher from Marple, a small village near Hyde in Cheshire. His formidable wife had ruthlessly driven her two sons through the state school system to obtain county council scholarships that had taken them up the tiny ladder of opportunity to Manchester University. And now he was studying at a London hospital on his way to qualifying as an FRCS, a modern version of Dick Whittington whose statue looked down on him kindly from the middle of the square, bag over shoulder. Ambrose could not help but be fascinated by the glitter: A young girl was getting out of a taxi, dressed up to the nines, followed by a rather austere looking woman with sharp eyes, dressed in black. The girl's look of expectation and excitement just transfixed him.

Although grand, it was not actually a full society ball. Mary Trevelyan's town house was not large enough, as her mother-in-law had impressed upon her. Her husband Sir Charles, third Baronet, was a junior government minister so the event had attracted Earl Grey, the foreign secretary and the German ambassador, but also there were some fellow Liberal MPs; Noel Buxton, rather swashbuckling in his own way, Leo Chiozza Money, a protégé of Lloyd George and Bertie Lees-Smith. There were also some intellectuals on the make, including Lily Widlake chaperoning the young Joyce Holman, her niece, to her first society event.

Lily thought it would be good for the girls. Percy, the older brother would be studying for his exams, of course. Her sister Emma, their mother, ruled out Christabel, because she was too young, so she had rushed upstairs in floods of tears. Maureen, the oldest, was just getting over a very bad cold so she could not go either.

"You get all the fun" she said rather nastily to Joyce, sensible enough not to reply and provoke the argument that would ground her. No, it would be a great occasion.

 Lily, a not quite suffragette headteacher, was soon engrossed, deep in conversation with Bertrand Russell. Drinks were being offered and he passed her a glass of champagne. Joyce was able to slip away to explore on her own. She went into the hall, watching new guests arriving.

She walked along a corridor and looked into the smoking room, the door of which was slightly ajar. She could see the back of a bald-headed man sitting near the door. That's a zero, she thought.

"Bertie. It's like a tinderbox over there. The slightest spark.." – but then she heard him speak.

"I think you exaggerate…" - alright, a two! Voice was a novel factor but somehow it remained with her. She passed into the main ballroom where couples were dancing to the band: they all looked so elegant, she thought. There was a young man with an older companion who was saying.

"You must join in, Siegfried."

The German ambassador caught 'Siegfried' and turned. "Are you over here for long?" He asked in perfect English.

"I live here, sir," he replied with pride.

"Then you are very lucky, I hope your luck will stay with you."

Joyce thought a five for the young man, perhaps more had he shown any interest in his surroundings or the opposite sex. Joyce was attempting dancing steps at the back of the ballroom when Count Nickolai Sambor almost burst into the room – at last here was a ten! Unfortunately, just behind him was a beautiful girl with long black hair and almost as much presence as he had. The Count apologised to Mary for being late and was forgiven on the promise of a dance. He introduced his daughter, Olga. Gosh, he's not bad at all, thought Joyce. In the smoking room the bald man got up and said he would have to circulate.

"You would win a contest for arguing," he said to Charles.

"Funny, I heard one of your students say the same thing, Bertie, yes you'd better go and join the party or I'll be in the doghouse."

He entered the ballroom. He saw the young girl dancing by herself, totally captivated by the event – so alive, Bertie felt. He passed on to chat to the intellectuals in the other room. The Count did dance with Mary and then explained that they would have to leave early to catch the boat train and then on to Frankfurt to see the family of Olga's fiance.

"But it will be the Sabbath by the time we get there," she said.

"They are very liberal Jews. Anyway nobody cares about that sort of thing anymore. We are in Western Europe," the Count replied.

"There you are," said Lily as she caught up with Joyce and Bertie had a glimpse of her being led away, protesting.

But there was something about the way she walked down the steps that stayed long in the memory.

A month later, Percy Holman had just graduated from the LSE. His parents had arranged a party and he was delivering invitations. He knocked on his tutor's door.

"Come in – oh it's you, Percy, congratulations it was nearly a first."

"But not quite, don't ever be happy with second best," came from a voice behind the door.

"This is Bertie Lees-Smith," said the tutor.

"You gave some of the best economics lectures on the course, professor...oh, yours were very good too, Mr Moore."

"It's Geoffrey now, you are no longer a student. What can I do for you? It can't be a late essay!"

"No, I've brought an invitation to my Graduation party."

"Gosh, sounds very formal."

"No, its drinks and canapes at my parents house in Highgate." Percy handed him the well-produced invitation.

"Your father is a printer, I see." said Geoffrey examining the card. "Yes, I'd be delighted to come – how about you Bertie? A bit of young company would do you good, come on, you'll like it".

Percy cut in. "I would be very honoured, professor."

"Well, alright, thanks. I'll try to get there, and I'm not a professor, at least not here; please call me Bertie." He shook Percy's hand.

"Have you invited Gunter? He is a bit out on a limb these days." Geoffrey asked.

"Already done," said Percy.

Alistair gently lifted the faded but impressive invitation card, edged in gold.

As so often in those days, there was yet another debate on Ireland. With over 90 MPs the Irish Home Rule Party, electoral allies of the ruling Liberal party, were hard to ignore, as was the traffic jam holding up Bertie's bus, caused by a vociferous demonstration of suffragettes, who had no MPs at all. He was sympathetic, although as a bachelor he had to admit to himself, not passionately so. Indeed, there was a distinct lack of passion in his life – was it a crime to feel the want of it? He was 44; there had been both means and opportunities. He had had a brilliant and varied academic career, rising to be the first professor of Political Economy at Bristol University, generously funded by Wills, the tobacco baron, and Bertie had been well rewarded - so well in fact, it had bankrolled his move into politics.

In 1910 he had been elected the second, then unpaid, Liberal MP for Northampton. An obscure by-product of the Peoples' budget of some significance to Bertie was that when he had been an MP for less than a year he got a handsome salary for the privilege.

As an MP he was invited to numerous soirees and balls like the Trevelyans. He had read somewhere that women were attracted to power, but that hadn't worked for him. Not that he had much! Now he really did have the means as well as opportunity. Oh dear, Bertie, you'll have to raise your game. And the bus had been stopped yet again, this time for a demonstration on behalf of striking dockers, represented more or less by the new Labour Party.

Luckily there was no attempt by the Conservative opposition to filibuster down the Irish bill by giving deliberately long speeches, so the house broke up early. Bertie went onto the House of Commons terrace and savoured a delicious port.

"You wouldn't be trying to influence a member of the Bar Committee with a free drink, would you? But this is rather nice," he said to Stanley Baldwin.

"I admit my motives are not entirely honest," said Stanley.

"Good. Then you'd better make it another one." Bertie put his hand in his pocket and felt Percy's invitation. He had been touched by the young man's sincerity – why not? "No, you owe me. I've got a date," said Bertie holding the card.

"Well Good Luck. You can invite me to the wedding."

"That would cost you a whole bottle of port," replied Bertie as he went off for a cab.

He arrived in Highgate only a few minutes late. It was a terraced house but very spacious inside. He was greeted by a young girl who took his hat and coat.

"Thank you..."

"Christabel," and she introduced him to her father Sidney.

"You're a printer?" Asked Bertie.

"Actually, I own a paper company."

"I'm sorry. Percy said you had printed your own invitations......

"Oh, Percy knows nothing about the nuts and bolts of life."

"Me neither," said Bertie.

"At least you've made a career of it." Said Sidney.

"You're only as good as your next election."

"Good business for us."

"I'll bear you in mind."

Sidney introduced Bertie to Emma, his wife, an attractive, feisty woman who nevertheless had her work cut out to keep tabs on Percy and his three younger sisters. He had already met the youngest, Christabel. Bertie noticed that Geoffrey, his colleague, had cornered the eldest sister, Marjorie. Be careful, he thought,

Geoffrey has a reputation. Still at 22 she should be able to hold her own, wasn't that what it was all about these days? Weren't women supposed to be independent? Gunter, Percy's fellow student, was eating a canapé on his own. Bertie went over and was saluted in the Prussian way.

"No need for that, Gunter, we're not in Heidelburg. Please call me Bertie."

"I'm from Frankfurt, Sir; just up the road."

"I loved Heidelburg. I gave a lecture there at the University. It was beautiful. Reminded me of Oxford."

"Old Frankfurt is very nice too. You must come over to visit."

"I'd love to. In the meantime, let's go out into the garden and listen to the German band. They do sound rather good."

Bertie was feeling so relaxed. He noticed a familiar young girl and walked over to her. "Joyce, isn't it, weren't you at the ball?"

She remembered his voice and got up. "Is it Bertie?"

"At your service. Are you free for the next dance?"

She was and Bertie found himself in the dance of his life . . .it was a Viennese waltz. He felt powerful and for once translated this into his feet. He could feel her responding. At the end he thanked her and bowed. She curtsied in reply. They had a drink and they found themselves talking and walking as if they were alone.

The evening was drawing to a close. The band leader announced the last waltz and it was Joyce who asked him for the dance.They got very close and at the end she kissed him, full on the lips. This was new for both of them.

In the morning, Joyce went to her mother and asked her if she could arrange to meet Bertie again. "Better than that, my dear. We'll have him round to dinner and then go and hear the talk of the town, Dr Hector Munro at the London Theosophical Society."

2 THE MANUSCRIPT

The large hall was packed to the rafters but they managed to get seats. The President introduced the Doctor, 'straight from the front line'. It was obvious that Hector Munro had never addressed such a large audience before. He started describing the walk along the shore by Dieppe, looking out over the salt marsh populated by thousands of wading birds. He thought he might have spotted an avocet. The President coughed politely.

Alistair picked up a thick manuscript titled M H H in large letters. Underneath were the letters J W.

It began with Hector's speech. He walked around the harbour. He had just sat down outside a cafe overlooking the pier with a croissant and cafe au lait. He was just savouring the smell of the coffee when a ferry landed and in a short time British soldiers disembarked, formed into ranks and marched off at a smart pace. He could see many more gathering on the deck waiting their turn. There was a sense of purpose that went well beyond normal parade drill. By the time he had drunk his coffee the ferry had been replaced by another. There were no civilian foot passengers. With his binoculars he could see other ships waiting out to sea. The BEF were landing.

Thinking that his vacation should be cut short, Hector went towards the railway station. He saw a man limping down the street on an improvised crutch. He had a leg wound that had been bandaged very roughly, to his professional eye. Further along there were other injured soldiers being carried in wheelbarrows, equally poorly bandaged. He turned the corner onto the large square in front of the station. It was a scene of horror. The wounded were lying in rows, often just on the cobbles, exposed to the sun. Although the square was almost filled with bodies, it was still and ghostly. Indeed some had passed away already. Instinctively Hector got out his medical bag and began to treat the worst cases in the immediate area. There did not seem to be anybody else trying to help. After a while he was aware of people carrying bodies to the other side of the square. He realised that another trainload of casualties had arrived. Eventually a man came over to talk to him. They took a much needed break in a cafe. In broken English the Frenchman introduced himself as Philippe Mareshal. He explained he was in fact a dentist, all the doctors and medical supplies had been sent to the front. Here all the bandages they had were provided by local women desperately cutting up their own sheets. The wounded were being evacuated as quickly as possible but there was no plan to deal with them here. Hector began to realise that there was much more to the panic. The Germans had broken through and were advancing rapidly. Trains for Paris were diverted. No wonder the Frenchman was so distressed and afraid.

Over the next couple of weeks Hector and the dentist did bring some kind of primitive order to the chaos. Buildings were requisitioned and the wounded were not left in the square; the trainloads of casualties still materialised but there was usually some warning. More doctors came to the rescue from the countryside.

The dentist said to Hector: "you've helped enough here. Go back and tell them what's happening."

Bertie's journal described the total silence when the speech finished. You could hear a pin drop. Then everyone stood up and cheered and cheered.

Dudley Wright was a friend of Emma's and had been present at the talk. He joined the Holmans for a drink with Bertie after the event.

Dudley was a senior London surgeon from the Metropolitan

Hospital. He was 47 but had gone to the War Office to join up. He had heard nothing so he went to the British Red Cross who suggested he go across to France himself with his own surgical team. Easier said than done!

Emma had already formed ideas for raising funds and Bertie would get some Liberal friends to support it. At least this is something positive I can do, he thought.

The next two weeks were feverishly busy. Never underestimate the power of Society women at this time. They had taken Hector Munro to their hearts, some of them very closely. In a mad rush of parties and fundraisers, the necessary cash had been raised to equip Dudley with an operating table, drugs and dressings. Emma Holman and her daughters, along with other Society Ladies all worked tirelessly. Bertie could not remember ever being as happy.

So it was that on a chilly morning in the middle of September there was a party on the platform of Victoria Station to see off Dudley and his initial team of other doctors and nurses including Barbara Mcglashan. In the party were Emma and Joyce. Then Bertie arrived just in time, running down the platform towards the cheering crowd. He almost lost his hat.

They watched the train depart. Just as they were leaving, Emma turned to Bertie and asked:

"What are your intentions?"

"To marry Joyce, if she'll have me." He heard himself blurt out. "That's clear enough," said Emma. "What do you think, my dear?"

She faced Joyce, who nodded slowly.

"Two years, Bertie, I'll give you two years. If you both feel the same, you can marry her then. Chaperone in the meantime." She swept off with her daughter leaving Bertie staring down at the empty tracks. 'Well, I suppose it's for the best.', he thought. Even so, two years seemed a long time.

The manuscript followed Dudley's progress. They had not been able to get through to Paris as they planned due to the German advance but the Mayor of Dieppe requisitioned the Hotel du Rhin for their use. 'At least we occupy some part of Germany now.'

One advantage of Dieppe was that communications with home could not be easier. With hindsight this might have been obvious but it made a great idea possible to realise. Volunteers and supplies poured in to support a hospital of sixty-five beds and a busy outpatient department.

Back in London the supporters realised that they had an ongoing job on their hands and under the new War Charities Act they decided to set up the Hospital Benevolent Society with Bertie as chairman. Armed with the regular reports from the new hospital in France, Bertie took a lead in fundraising in his constituency in Northampton. He formed a truce with Parker, the Conservative mayor, and together they toured local factories and church halls, raising a lot of money and weekly subscriptions.

Early next year with much hooting, a large car drew up across the street from the Hotel Du Rhin. It was the Vicomtesse de la Panousse, the head of the French Red Cross. She swept into the reception accompanied by her liveried chauffeur. Dudley showed her round and took her to his office.

"This place is marvellous. You are doing a brilliant job but..." she paused.

"But?" Dudley looked at her intently.

"But you need proper buildings to expand. You can expand?"'

Dudley nodded. "I believe so, yes, I'm sure we can. I'll get in touch with the committee."

"The military position had stabilised. If you say yes, we have a much better building in Yvetot," said the Vicomtesse.

"Yvetot?"

"You won't have heard of it but it's a small market town twenty-five miles away between Le Havre and Rouen. If you agree we'll call it Hopital de l'Alliance. I will drive you there now."

"And I will buy you lunch, Mademoiselle."

"Enchantee!"

They were driven through the French countryside. Although he had walked along the seafront many times, Dudley had not ventured much further. He had feared it would be too depressing. Part of the journey was through a small town that had been briefly occupied by the Germans and then regained. It was badly damaged and the people looked very dispirited.

"We are fighting back." The Vicomtesse said angrily.

They reached Yvetot and drove up to a substantial detached house in the middle of the town. It had large wings and a formal garden. "This will be your hospital," announced the Vicomtesse.

They went in and inspected the elegant but empty interior of the main house. "This was the Jesuit College - Guy de Maupassant was educated here."

Dudley could not believe it. "My people have estimated you could have two hundred beds here." The Vicomtesse continued.

"Yes," was all Dudley could say. "Yes, I suppose you could."

Alistair picked up Bertie's journal.

On the outbreak of war, Charles Trevelyan had resigned from the government and formed the Union for Democratic Control, a pressure group campaigning for peace by a negotiated settlement. They were also critical of government moves such as conscription.

Bertie was on the committee, as was Bertrand Russell. In the midst of all this, he could not be happier. His relationship with the Holmans had blossomed, he had never experienced a family Christmas before. He had a real respect for Emma and Sydney and had got to know Percy and the other sisters a lot better. The relationship with Joyce was... well, going along slowly, he thought. He found the chaperoning irksome but Joyce did not seem to mind as much. Usually Aunt Lily, the redoubtable headmistress, played the role, somewhat too enthusiastically for his liking. Sometimes he felt as if he was treading water but his feelings for Joyce did not diminish. He was a determined but patient man, accustomed to getting his way eventually by gentle persuasion. Above all, perhaps, he did not know what Joyce was thinking, let alone feeling, although she was always studiously polite. They still went to dances but there were no more German bands and the Vienna waltz but a distant memory.

Early in 1915, Bertie received an invitation from the Red Cross to go to the new hospital in France. Parker would accompany him and Bertie asked Percy if he would like to come along; like every young man, Percy was under tremendous pressure to join up. He had received his share of white flowers but he wanted to work out his position for himself. It would be a good experience to go over and he accepted the invitation with alacrity.

With difficulty they arrived at Yvetot, which was much grander than they imagined. They were accompanied by Philippe Mareshal, the dentist, who offered to act as a translator. Bertie had never been round any hospital before so it all seemed very clean and efficient. All the patients were French soldiers but he managed to converse reasonably well. Some patients stayed to convalesce; others were discharged and sent home; more were transferred to bigger hospitals and a few died. However neat and well managed it was, the scale of casualties was overwhelming; every couple of days the empty beds were filled; it did not require much imagination to realise 100 other hospitals were doing the same thing further along the front, and then another 100 and then yet more.. Some of the casualties were in a terrible state and during the week they were there they did observe some deaths and attended a funeral in the church on the other side of the square.

 It was much more shocking than he thought. There seemed no chance for Bertie to get to the Front; he could see enough here in the hospital At least he got to know Percy. It was hard to move from pupil to prospective brother-in-law. Irrespective of that, he was a serious young man, as vulnerable as anybody else to pressure to join up and ... well, become a patient like this... in a hospital like this... if he was lucky.

Percy was standing outside having a cigarette, a rare treat, but he felt he needed it.

"You're not used to this, are you?" He turned round to see a young nurse, slightly taller than himself.

"No, you're right, I'm not. How on earth do you cope?"

"I don't really; we keep busy with rigid routines, in part to protect ourselves."

"Does it work?"

"Most of the time. I'm Dorothy Anderson, by the way, I work here with my sister Mosa."

"And I'm Percy Holman." He paused. "Please let me buy you a drink when you come off duty."

They were just about to leave when Dudley heard a familiar hooting, as the Vicomtesse de la Panousse arrived. She swept in, gathered everybody together in the former school hall and gave an impassioned speech. Much of the French was lost to Bertie but at the end he was motioned to come forward and the Vicomtesse pinned the Legion d'Honneur on his chest. There was a lot of clapping. No need to go to the Front now, I've received my medal; and Percy had got his girl.

Well it's worth a few drinks at the club, Bertie mused in the taxi back to Dieppe - even Joyce might be impressed. Philippe looked pensive and said to Bertie

"You are an MP."

"Yes, unless things have changed drastically at home."

"You had better look at this."

Philippe had a word with the taxi driver and a large sum of money changed hands. They diverted to the right and then towards the Belgian border. They took country lanes to avoid road blocks and managed to enter the British Sector undetected. Philippe directed the driver to a small chateau.

"Wait here," he said.

After a few minutes he returned with a young English doctor. They got into the taxi. The man looked totally exhausted.

Bertie said. "I'm an MP and still can ask the government difficult questions. But I need facts. Whatever you say will be treated with the utmost confidence."

"You can see for yourself if you are quick. All the army personnel have gone back to HQ for a briefing and a good meal, no doubt!"

The doctor took them round the wards. The first and abiding impression for the visitors was chaos. Actually there were no wards as such, just a collection of patients strewn about the rooms and corridors, apparently untreated and certainly uncared for. There were no nurses, just local French cleaners who did their best, a total contrast to the order and cleanliness of Yvetot.

"Casualties arrive every day. Sometimes they are just left outside. Nobody wants to come in here." There was a silence.

"The few drugs that reach here are strictly rationed by the army. I suspect some find their way to the black market. Worse still the army should have no say in critical clinical decisions such as whether a man should be sent back to Britain or return to the front. They don't like the expense of the former and I'm sure they have targets for the latter."

As they left Bertie was deeply depressed by what he saw. But it would not be easy to return to Dieppe as they had already broken every rule in the book just by being there. Philippe stopped the taxi, reached into his pocket and attached a Red Cross pennant to the front wing. This worked wonders until the outskirts of Dieppe where military police questioned them more thoroughly. Luckily Hotel du Rhin was still functioning as a hospital so Philippe managed to convince them that their visit had been something to do with that.

Bertie and Percy thanked Philippe and said farewell as they caught the ferry back to Newhaven. The sea was calm but grey as they stood on deck. Bertie turned to Percy.

"Can I share my thoughts with you?"

"Of course."

"This affects you possibly more than me. The British Army is growing massively, one day we had over 30,000 volunteers, that's more than the size of the British Army at Waterloo. There is a sinister alliance between the Army who want battalions and the Liberal Government who want to avoid conscription. I have met these men. They want numbers, no questions asked. Someone had the idea of the Pals Battalions, you will hear much more about them. And the Government wants Shells and more Shells…

What they fail to see is casualties on any scale. That is obvious from what we have just seen. Yes, I will ask a question in Parliament but I've never seen the Government so strong and self-assured. If nothing comes of my question, I'm thinking of joining up." Percy looked totally shocked.

"Oh, I'm eligible, just!"

"Does Joyce know?" He said.

"No, and she must not: this has to be my decision. What about yourself?"

"What do you mean?"

"Do you want to join up?"

"I've been thinking of nothing else since War broke out. Of course the family want me to complete my studies. I assumed that's what you thought."

"Yes and No. They certainly haven't consulted me and I wouldn't say anything anyway. But if it helps what I can probably do is offer you a chance to serve in the Medical Corps. It will be no picnic as we saw but that's where I'll be going."

 Percy looked towards the Dover cliffs. Bertie knew this was a life changing moment as he gazed with him.

"Yes." He said at length. "Yes, please help me to join the Medical Corps."

3 COMMITMENT

Bertie had asked a nuanced Parliamentary Question that did not seem to draw any reaction from the Government. What did he expect? So he took the next step. This was what his constituents did every day. Of course he could claim exception as an MP. He was 44 and asthmatic, not good military material - perhaps they'll reject me out of hand.

He walked to the Recruiting Office and joined the queue. There were men of all ages from all walks of life. Some looked very young indeed, a few older than he. Some were friends. He felt very moved. This was the genuine People's Army and he felt honoured to be joining.

Eventually his turn came. The young clerk did not look up. Name… Age… Occupation: Member of Parliament. The young man continued to write. Then he stopped.

"You must be having me on." Then he looked up and his mouth opened wide. "You really are the MP."

There was a silence around the hall. An Officer got up and sauntered across. "What are you doing here?"

"I'm joining up like all these other good people." There was a huge spontaneous cheer as people realised what was happening. Bertie knew he had done the right thing.

That evening it was his turn to be behind the bar. One member quipped. "Doing some honest work at last, eh Bertie." Try as he might, the apron did not suit him. Ian Macpherson, the Under Secretary of State for War, stood in front of him.

"What have you done, Bertie?"

"I've joined up."

"I know that but why?" Ian said, who previously had put him down as a rebel, if not a coward. "If this is a trick, Bertie, it's a dangerous one. I'm not sure what I can do."

"I don't want you to get me off. I do not want to serve as an officer but I do want to serve as a stretcher bearer at the Front, no favourable treatment. Oh, there is just one. My fiancee's brother plans to enlist soon. Please let him have the choice of serving in the Medical Corps." "'No problem. Give me his name," he paused. "Oh and I did take note of your question on the Medical Corps and indeed of your little jaunt by the Belgian border. I can see you are serious. I underestimated you. You're a brave man. Good Luck."

Bertie smiled. "I could not possibly comment."

Ian shook Bertie's hand.

"My son has gone to France as well. I'm afraid to say I did try to stand in his way."

"I hope he survives."

Now for the big test. He sent a card to the Holmans asking to see them that evening. Unusually the door was opened by a maid who ushered him into the drawing room where the family were waiting. He was never quite sure how they knew something important was about to happen but there was an almost tangible air of expectation.

Looking round, he said. "There is no easy way to say this but I have joined up." There was an audible gasp...and then silence.

"Did you receive a white flower?" Someone said.

"No. Percy may have told you but on our way back to Dieppe we diverted to see a British Casualty Hospital which was truly dreadful. I asked a Parliamentary Question which was fobbed off so now I feel I have to take the next step. I will be a stretcher bearer."

"Not an Officer?"

"No, that was as far as my conscience would take me. I will at least have a better idea of what is happening out there. I have one other thing to say. It's no secret that sooner or later, conscription will be introduced, so I have asked that when his time comes, Percy will have the same choice as me to serve in the Medical

Corps…if he so wishes. There's no hurry, Percy: I just wanted to give you the chance."

"I'll go," said Percy. "You've been a great help. You have saved me a lot of heartsearching."

Sidney got up. "Bertie, I want to thank you very much on behalf of the family, especially Percy. Now I'm going to ask Joyce to accompany you onto the terrace, where I'm sure you have a lot to talk about." Emma stared at him, about to say something but remained silent.

Joyce went through to the terrace. Bertie followed her. Before he could say anything, she kissed him right on the lips. Bertie was overwhelmed. "Will you marry me?" He asked.

"Ask me properly." She replied. The door was ajar and Emma could not resist following them. She saw Bertie on his knees and heard a firm 'Yes' from her daughter. It was to be.

On a crisp morning in September, a year after he had seen off Dudley's train on Victoria Station, Bertie took the branch line to Aldershot barracks, where he was to receive the basic month's military training for a private in the Royal Army Medical Corps. This time there was a list and it was much more formal, almost forbidding. Popular or not, the Army was determined to impose it's particular stamp. In a very short time he had been sworn in, given a uniform and ordered to form up with twenty others. The Sergeant came across and walked up and down the line. He was authoritative but not unkindly. "Welcome to the British Army. I know you are volunteers and think you are going to save lives. I hope you do. I know you will do your best. This training is to help you save your own life. Do not underestimate what you are about to undertake. But if you survive, others will too. Good Luck!"

He then handed over to a corporal who shouted at them and made them run around the barracks square. His fellow recruits were all unfit, wherever they had come from. Bertie got to know them a lot better over the next four weeks and he had to admit that whatever the methods, they were all much fitter, above all much more cohesive as a group. The training came to an end and Bertie was pleased to learn that they were all to be sent out together to join the same unit in France.

They had three days leave before they departed and Bertie had an appointment he had to keep in Grosvenor Square.

Joyce was the first of Emma's daughters to marry and despite herself, she had got very excited by the detail. They had little enough time of course, but she and Joyce had chosen a lovely dress. Emma thought she was still far too young to get married, but circumstances had forced the event, as happened so often in those days. Still Grosvenor Chapel was a fine Church. There would be no honeymoon, Bertie was only on leave for three days. Due to his position, the event attracted a lot of attention and the family found themselves in the news for the first time. There were some faded press articles. The guest list was unbalanced; the Holmans turned up in force - Bertie's two brothers attended, both very different. Harry tried unsuccessfully to seduce Marjorie and Emma found Arthur praying outside the reception.

"There was no need for that," said Bertie to his brother Harry, more in sorrow than anger.

"I didn't mean to spoil the show, too much of your nice bitter. Congratulations, by the way, she is a lovely girl."

"Keep your hands off."

"No, I know I would get a good slap. I'm off to South Africa by the way." "You're going with Arthur to join the Salvation Army - Alleluya!"

"Not exactly, I've got a golden opportunity in the mines."

"Why don't you take this dish to help you pan."

"No, I'm head of the Mining Police."

"That will be just beer money, then." They clinked glasses. "You will want to settle down some day, we all do."

Bertie caught up with Percy. "I'm really sorry about my brother."

"I really don't mind people praying, perhaps more of us should do it these days."

"You know I didn't mean that one."

"Well, actually, I'm more worried about Marjorie and Geoffrey. I very much regret ever giving an invitation to him, I did have a bad feeling about him."

"Well, you must learn to trust your feelings - last lecture, you're my brother now. Harry is off to South Africa as well as Arthur. I'm glad you brought Dorothy along, though."

"Mosa is getting along rather well with the Buxtons, who is that other girl they brought along?" Percy asked.

"Oh, you stick with Dorothy, you'd never keep up with Eglantine Jebb."

Meanwhile Dorothy was getting the third degree from Emma and Joyce. She had already got a first from Cambridge which, as Emma wisely remarked, was a long way from Basutoland where she was born. Aunt Lily congratulated Joyce. "You can hold your own balls now." She said.

"Maybe not quite yet." Replied Joyce.

The guests included some fellow MPs, all rather grand, especially Charles Trevelyan and his wife, Mary. Stanley arrived with a whole case of best Port. "How on earth did you get that through the blockade. Don't tell me." Asked Bertie.

"Life can be good from another side."

"Stanley, this stuff is so good I would be willing to defect. But it would cost you at least another case."

"I'll see what I can do." Stanley replied.

The party agent and Jessie Finch, the Liberal Chairman from Northampton, were there, as were some fellow recruits, who really did look lost. Sidney ensured that alcohol was provided in large quantities and a very good party ensued, the details of which remained vague for many. Everybody had the port for the final toast and afterwards the guests all went their very separate ways.

Bertie was lying in bed with a sore head the morning after. He could not believe that it had all happened. He was lying back luxuriating in the silk sheets after the more austere conditions in the barracks. He stretched his arm across to his wife to find her half of the bed empty. Joyce walked out of the bathroom. "Wake up. Bertie, we're going out." This had not been on his immediate agenda but none the less he made plans to get up. After a few minutes he heard Joyce say. "We're meeting Mother at nine." He did like his mother-in-law but perhaps not right now on this honeymoon of a day. Over breakfast Joyce explained that in Bertie's absence, the charity had continued successfully to raise money but as the war ground on, the need for long term rehabilitation at home for some of the rising number of casualties had become clear. It had been decided to refocus the charity towards building a facility here in London... and they were going to look at some sites. "What is going to happen to Yvetot?"

"It is going to be handed over to the French Red Cross as a working hospital, along with the money already collected."

"Oh, does that mean I lose the Legion d'Honneur?"

"Don't be silly, Bertie. Look, I'm not interested in that. I just want you to come back in one piece." said Joyce, kissing him across the table.

"I'm going to have some more champagne." said Bertie. "I need it!"

The M H H manuscript continued the story.

They were joined by Sir William Younger and Theodore Carr who were helping to bankroll the whole show. After looking at several sites, Bertie's enthusiasm was beginning to wane. Thank God for my army training or I'd be on the floor by now, he thought. They were revived by a good lunch including some Younger's beer at the Spaniards on Hampstead Heath. They were telling Peter, the landlord, that they had run out of sites. He thought for a moment. "There's the Manor House just over the hill," he said. So will I be, thought Bertie. "The old lady has just died and there's no family. It's a bit run down, of course."

They went along the North End Road and down towards Golders Green. They stopped in the road opposite Anna Pavlova's House. The entrance was in a recess in the wall. Joyce rang the bell. An elderly manservant opened a creaking door. Is this a melodrama, Bertie thought, or have I just had too much to drink? They went down a dimly lit passage.

Alistair remembered the passage, the marble floor in the old manor house, the palm court with the fountain and small garden. There were fourteen acres with fine old trees: A little Park next to the Heath.

Sir William said. "I believe there are secret passages leading up Hampstead Hill."

"Do they come out anywhere near the Spaniards?" Bertie asked. "Privileged information, Bertie." Sir William replied. "Talking of which, aren't you on the House of Commons committee that decides which beers are sold in the bar?"

"Not to mention the biscuits." said Carr.

"I couldn't possibly comment." said Bertie.

The place was perfect. The government requisitioned Hampstead Hill and numbers of temporary hospital buildings rapidly began to appear as the Manor House Hospital was born.

M H H.

4 THE BIG PUSH

Bertie got off the train at Aldershot into the driving rain and was soon back in the swing of things. There were no secrets in the group. The closest recruit to him in occupation was a teacher; there was an engineer who had been a shop steward, and a footman, a draper and many others. He got to know their stories... and they got to know his. Their motivation was extremely varied. The teacher was there because of Belgium; the shop steward because his employer had pressured him to go... and Bertie... well because he wanted to find out more... that all seemed very thin now. But he had set himself a challenge and knew he must not back down. They all had expressed a desire to be in the Medical corps rather than to fight directly. The army had respected their wishes. That said, Bertie had to admit that the training had welded them together as well as anything he had ever experienced.

They set off for France. Train to Newhaven. Ferry to Dieppe. Bertie had a sense of deja vue, but they turned north-east to a hospital some ten miles from the front. It, too, was in a chateau but with a large number of tents in the grounds. Each of the twenty was assigned to work with an experienced orderly who would show them what to do. The first task was to empty the ambulances, which could be motorised or horse drawn. All of the wounds were horrendous, sometimes men were piled on top of one other. Each was assigned a bed but officers had their own ward. Occasionally there were dead bodies on the ambulances but generally the dying stayed at the casualty clearing stations, closer to the line.

The dead were buried in a small but growing cemetery on the other side of the woods. There was some dignity shown in the brief Anglican burial service that had to be attended by at least the two coffin bearers and one other. The service did not have to be carried out by a priest or padre. In fact the teacher developed a skill for conducting such services. Occasionally priests did attend. Even more occasionally the bodies of civilians, or some soldiers, if they had identified as Catholics, were sent to the local church. Bertie was not used to funerals and found the whole scene macabre but what was the alternative?

It was on the living the hospital concentrated. He had little medical knowledge but he could see that the staff made an enormous effort to save lives. He brought in soldiers who at first glance had no chance. They were patched up and looked after round the clock. Most responded well to the good care and food provided. Many of the more seriously ill patients were sent back to Britain, as well as others who needed to convalesce for some time. Although the hospital was under a constant strain from the number of casualties, this was an immense improvement on his last visit to a British Hospital. Bertie was impressed with the efficiency with which it fulfilled its role. An efficiency he had to get right into on the double. Although he did not have servants as such, he was used to the services of a housekeeper and was not in the habit of undertaking domestic or any other form of manual labour. Very soon he was performing all the menial tasks in the hospital. His training in England had been mainly aimed at achieving a level of fitness and discipline. This he now found essential. He was subject to orders from a range of people, including female nurses. Most treated him with some respect but a small number did not and one or two were downright bullies. There was a theoretical appeal through his military line of command but Bertie realised he would have to fight his own battles. Ironically one of the worst bullies was a nurse who looked after the medicines from the basement of the chateau. Bertie was sure it had been a dungeon in former times. This nurse made him sweep the floor every time he came near; he felt sure it was to wipe away his own pollution. Eventually she left him alone, or rather picked on some other poor sod. Anyway Bertie coped well with the physical side. He had not been this fit for at least twenty years. Perhaps he was better military material than he had thought. He slept extremely well and he was almost enjoying the whole job. Using his body not his brain he was surprised how rapidly he got used to the unpleasant sides of his job: the blood; the soiling; the dying, He just dealt with it by cleaning, boiling and carrying. Carrying. His chosen weapon of war was the Army Mark 1 Stretcher. With regulation sheet and blanket (shroud for a corpse). You might not think there was a skill to carrying a stretcher but experienced hands will tell you different. And Corporal John Dyer, Bertie's mentor, was just such an experienced hand. In civilian life, John had been a postman, so he was fitter than most. He had left school at fourteen and was now barely twenty but Bertie could see how intelligent he was. Anyway John chose Bertie and they got on like the proverbial house on fire. Truth be told working for John (always Corporal) was the best part of the day.

Or nearly. There was the letter from home. Joyce and Bertie wrote to each other every day, although the letters did not necessarily arrive in order. Both were shy at first, feeling each other out, but gradually the relationship grew as they took strength from each other.

After a month the unit was given orders to move on. As the British Army expanded, it took over new sections of the front to the south, as much as twenty miles at a time. This freed the French to supply more men to defend Verdun. To support the troops, new field hospitals were requisitioned and forward Casualty Clearing Stations had to be set up behind the new line. Bertie's unit was sent to one of these.

The weather had distinctly worsened. Bertie had asked for socks and warm clothing to be sent. These he shared with Corporal John and the rest of the unit. They needed all the protection they could get. The new location was not only much colder but closer to the front line. In fact if you took a not very long walk to the top of the hill you could see it about half a mile away. The ground they stood on was a section of the line that the Germans had retreated from after the battle of the Marne. The

French had pushed them back over the hill, so it formed part of a small salient that the Germans wanted back. Whoever chose the location must have come on a quiet day, because there was sporadic shelling when the Germans overshot. Everything of value, including the patients, had to be protected behind mounds of earth to minimise splinter damage. There was more attention by enemy aeroplanes who seemed oblivious to the large red crosses prominent on the top of the tents. The clearing station was all tents, so there was little protection against the cold and the damp, except it was surrounded by forests. Not quite in a clearing - the wits wondered if the officer in charge of positioning the clearing station had interpreted his orders too literally - the trees did offer some protection from the wind, albeit that they were intersected by roads.

More than the relative discomfort, Bertie had a bad feeling about the place. Although he believed in God and belonged to the Church of England, he was not superstitious but there was definite sense of menace here and it concerned the unit and him personally.

They were very busy setting everything up. He was again impressed that by hard work and good organisation something so effective could be built so rapidly. It seemed that way to Bertie anyhow, who had not seen a clearing station before. However Corporal John had and even he was satisfied. There was time to make themselves reasonably comfortable with windbreaks, a decent washhouse and latrine. They had been lucky because the Germans did not seem to have noticed the change of enemy or taken advantage to cause more casualties.

Again Bertie had a sense of achievement. John came up to him and said. " Well, they've made me a Sergeant."

Bertie looked disappointed because they would not now be in such close day-to-day contact.

"But you won't get rid of me that easily. They've made you a Corporal." Bertie did not know what to think.

John and Bertie were granted a day's leave in the local town to celebrate. Bertie was looking forward to relaxing as they hitched a lift. The town appeared completely ruined. Bertie looked at John. He nodded grimly. They got out and walked down what had been the main street, now empty. A lot of the buildings had been destroyed by shellfire.

"This way, I believe." Said John. They went down a side street where there were steps down to a cellar. With a bar. And a barmaid. Both seemed very attractive in the dim candlelight. John bought Bertie a drink. It was a rather strong red wine, surprisingly fine, as was the whole atmosphere down here. Bertie began to relax. There was even a fire going. When he got used to the light, Bertie could see that there were other cellars interconnecting, all full of soldiers. They heard the sound of Cwm Rhondda through the passage.

John said. "Things must be bad."

"I think they sound rather good," said Bertie.

"No, that's not what I mean. They've got fresh uniforms. They're going to the Front."

"Troops must come and go," said Bertie.

"No, this is different. There's going to be a Big Push."

"A big push?" Asked Bertie, slow on the uptake.

"Yes, I saw it on some orders lying around. That's why we're up here so close to the Front. And there'll be volunteers for forward duty."

"I'm going where you go."

"You don't understand, Bertie, it's not for you."

"Look I'm very stubborn. I'm going if it happens. You've been here before, haven't you? Tell me about it, after I get us another drink, no arguing, I got promoted too."

Bertie got the drinks in somewhat halting French. The barmaid understood his needs all too well. It's a pity I've just got married, he thought. The warm atmosphere and the second large glass of wine worked well and John told his story.

"There was no organisation back then, we were attached to the Battalion. The walking wounded were treated just behind forward positions. There was no front line as such. A fluid one at best. It was all very gentlemanly. They would just wait for a ceasefire and then send in the stretcher bearers to collect the wounded. Then they treated the casualties wherever they could. Nobody expected such numbers. Even then there was no way we could pick up everybody who fell in the time we had. The Germans were doing the same. We got to know some of them. But there was always some hero who wanted to take a potshot, exact his own revenge. We fell back and back....and then suddenly we advanced, roughly to the present line. They began to set up proper Field Hospitals and Clearing stations. That's fine for day to day. Yes, men get hit but they're in our trench. Until a big push. I was at Loos six months ago. This time we're in the forward trenches. The whistles blow, the men go up ladders and disappear. You'll see. We're meant to stay back to locate casualties to pick up behind the second wave. Except there is no second wave The first wave is stuck out there on the wire. There was no wire there before, see... but now there is. And we don't know where it is or where the mines are, cos' it's been French. Anyway they gave up in the afternoon and raised a ceasefire flag. The Germans stuck to it. Why they did, I don't know because it was all our men out there. All along the front stretcher parties raced forward. The Germans respected that. Even collected some of ours near their trench. Saved their lives. We did not race for long. It was absolute slaughter, Bertie." He stopped. His friend was almost crying.

"Go on." said Bertie softly.

"It really was hell on earth. There was still the odd bullet and shell but that was nothing. I don't know which was worse: seeing fresh young men younger than me in bits from the shells or the mines. I'd seen that before. I hadn't seen men on the wire hanging like scarecrows, their uniforms shot off. But I could not believe how many were still surviving, begging for water, asking for their mothers. Brave men. I'm glad I did not have a revolver because I would have shot a lot of them. Put them out of their misery; court martial or not. Some did risk it. Again there was no way we could pick everybody up. The further towards the Germans they'd got, the harder it was to get to them. Poor buggers. The ceasefire gradually came to an end with an increase of fire from both sides. Many stretcher bearers bought it too. The next day was the same but shorter. But in the ceasefire there was the lonely sound of bagpipes. Then we were sent back to help deal with those we had managed to bring out. That is a Big Push."

Bertie went to get another drink. As he was waiting he looked around. Another Welsh hymn was being sung in the background. All these men will soon be lucky to survive. He felt real fear because he knew it also applied to John and himself. The next drinks were served by the patron. They were both silent and drank slowly.

The sergeant went on. "There were so many wounded we took them to the railhead. The platform was very long so that a lot of soldiers could be moved easily. Starting at one end we lay the unconscious wounded down side by side. A Doctor leant over to examine the bodies and assess the main problem. Then they got a nurse to attach a large square piece of paper to the uniform, on their chest, what was left of it, There were neat capital letters: G for Gangrene, E for eye and so on. It looked very tidy and clinical. When the platform was filled, we stopped for a cup of tea. I looked back at the line of bodies. None of them were moving. It was eerie. It was so quiet; yet turn round and the orderlies and nurses were relaxing and joking amongst themselves. The doctor was smoking and looking away, I remember. I heard later that someone had swapped their 'E' for the 'G' on the body next to him. God knows where he ended up."

"We'd better be going or we'll miss our transport." John said. He has aged ten years, Bertie thought. He could not believe the strong respect and, yes, love he felt for this man. They took in the dimly lit cellar for the last time and climbed the stairs to breathe in the cold evening air. The pissoir was undamaged.

As they walked back, the sergeant said: "Bertie, we were wrong about you. No, let me finish. We all thought this was a publicity stunt for you to boost your career."

"My career is... not worth the candle, I'm afraid; I visited a British hospital in the early days and was appalled. I asked a question in Parliament and was fobbed off so I thought I'd do it the hard way. As you say, things have improved but I think they are only beginning to look at what to do with large numbers of casualties... which could happen quite soon," said Bertie looking around. Yes, I could've ducked it but I'm bloody-minded so here I am. The army were right about one thing. I thought I would be too old and asthmatic, but I'm fine. You are young though."

"Not any more, I'm not," said John. And sadly it was true.

There was a nice picture of Bertie and his unit looking relaxed somewhere on the Somme.

They did not stay relaxed for long. Nothing was said about the Big Push. John said there was no point until it was necessary. Then he would give every man the chance to stay behind. There would be work enough wherever you were. When the time came John laid down what would happen if you were at the front. Everybody listened quietly. There was no pressure but almost everybody did volunteer. Bertie was not surprised. The Unit had come a long way. Bertie got his wish to serve with John. "No heroics, mind," he said smiling.

That evening they set off for the trenches over the hill. It was a cold winter evening but clear with a watery moon. They marched in full uniform, helmets, stretchers and Red Cross armbands. They looked so much better than when they had first started around the barracks in Aldershot. They now marched with purpose. As one.

They got to a ruined farmhouse. It was the entry point. There was a narrow slit trench that went towards the front line and eight men went along with five stretchers and one spare. Nobody asked what they were to do with the spare. The other members of the unit fanned out towards similar entry points to the right and left. Bertie climbed down a wooden ladder. The trench was initially about five feet deep. It was very dark now but Bertie could just see the broad shoulders of the sergeant walking steadily in front of him. Suddenly there was a huge explosion and a light flare went up. It was like daylight. Bertie crouched down at first but then looked out. He could see devastation on a vast scale, like some medieval painting he had seen but much worse; there was no hope here at all. He could pick out shell holes in shadows and even strands of barbed wire. The horror of what John had described in the cellar came back instantly. "Come on, Bertie, we can't stop here," came from in front.

More shells came over but the trench got deeper so you could not see over the top. 'Good thing', thought Bertie, never expecting to feel warm and protected in a trench. 'I suppose that's what they're for.' He thought. The barrage was building up and it was impossible to count the number of explosions. He heard a slightly different bang and realised that it was from the Germans returning fire. Aiming straight at him. He did not panic because he realised there was absolutely nothing he could do. But he understood men who did; men driven mad by the shells; they dealt with them every day. Previously all he had known directly was the occasional inaccurate German fire that peppered the clearing station. Now he hoped for a lot more inaccuracy. The trench twisted and turned so that if a shell did land close or in it, only a small part would be affected. Bertie did not find this reassuring. Eventually they came to a T-junction and Bertie realised this was the Front Line. Intermittently he could see like daylight because of the flares and he noticed the trench was deeper and wide enough for people to pass. He instinctively felt less protected. "Stay there." John said as he went to find his opposite number in the Keighley Pals.

They came back and the new sergeant showed them into what seemed to Bertie like a cave. "You can sleep here." Dimly Bertie could see other men round the sides and he lay down in a gap. It was very uncomfortable on the hard earth but Bertie was much more aware of the flashes, the noise of explosions and shaking of the floor and walls as shells exploded very close. It all merged into one continuous noise that just went straight through him as he fell asleep exhausted.

When he woke it was silent and very dark. He was incredibly stiff. No shells. Then someone came into the cave. "Wake up, Bertie, I've let you sleep long enough." John came in with a candle. All the others had disappeared.

"They're ready to go over the top," Said John. At the time the phrase had not the impact that it had later, so Bertie did not grasp it's full meaning. They went outside. The light was increasing all the time. From inside, the trench seemed well built like a battlement of a wooden castle. Sandbags added to the defensive height. The trench zigzagged, but at the end to the right was an observation point, with a wooden floor raised from the level of the trench, which Bertie now noticed had large puddles in places. Stout wooden ladders lay along the walls to the right and left. He shivered but there was a lot of activity going on as the men were making their final preparations for battle. Most were busying themselves with routine tasks. Some were openly praying. Others were smoking and staring into space. The sergeant was keeping a watchful but kindly eye. It was difficult to tell if anybody had done this before. Bertie thought it would have made little difference if they had. He looked around and realised that many of the young men in front of him would not return and the lives of those that did would be changed forever.

The Captain sauntered round the corner on the right, deliberately slowly, Bertie felt. But it was effective. The men stood to; he waved them to their ease, said firmly, "Good Luck, men." And started to climb the ladder in the middle. He looked at his watch, got out a whistle and blew it. Then he disappeared over the top of the parapet.

Other whistles could be heard clearly. All the men scrambled up and followed the Captain. There were no stragglers and the sergeant walked back down the trench to check the section round the corner. He would be the last man to go. John went to the observation post and skilfully placed a mirror on a stick so that he could see over the sandbags. The level of noise was steadily increasing as German shells began to fall and British guns fired back in reply. Then there was the unmistakable ratatat of a machine gun. Bertie could not believe how fast it sounded. The Sergeant motioned him over and handed him the stick with the mirror on. Very quickly he could see the battlefield. It seemed like total desolation yet there was a lot going on. The troops had advanced several hundred yards. He realised afterwards holes had been cut in the wire on the British side to allow troops through. The bombardment had created more holes in the German wire. The men were pouring through these. But the machine guns were concentrating on these gaps. Some men were already stuck on the wire. He could see the Captain far in the distance waving the men on. The machine gun in front of them suddenly stopped. Were they changing ammunition or had the gun jammed – life hung on such chances. Just then a British shell fell short and obliterated the leading party in a large cloud. Bertie strained to see what happened but there was too much smoke. All he thought he could make out was the shape of a horseman.

"I think the Captain's down but the machine gun is jammed."

"You think, you think...you think too much," said John, grabbing the mirror stick. But then he said. "Yes, you're right… sorry Bertie. Are you up for this? Let's go now."

Bertie nodded and they went over the top with the stretcher. There was another team left in the trench to take the casualty into the relative safety of one of the 'caves'. They would hand another stretcher back and then the top team would go forward to pick up another man. It worked better than Bertie had imagined for the first few casualties close to the trench. But the further away they got the longer it took and the more danger they were in. It might be obvious what they were doing but there was no ceasefire and attitudes were hardening on both sides. But their luck held a while longer. The attack was broken and the men were drifting back, taking full advantage of the jammed machine gun. A padre had now joined them giving the last rights and tending to men who were dying but also welcoming and encouraging the men back to the safety of the British trench. Men who had already returned were helping bring their comrades back in. Bertie was not sure how long he could go on but he was still noticing everything that was happening. However the Germans were now directing increasingly accurate rifle fire at the fleeing enemy. Reluctantly John and Bertie were forced to stop.

Next morning John woke Bertie very early. "I'm sorry about this, please keep it to yourself."

5 A SHOOTING

They drove to a building that had clearly been a school but was now the local battalion headquarters, a mile behind the front.

"We'll stay here," said John, as they walked into a walled school yard at the back. They had not long to wait. At 5 o'clock sharp the door opened and an officer marched out, followed by six soldiers with rifles. Behind them two more soldiers were dragging a man forward – bringing up the rear was a Church of England padre. He did have a prayer book open but appeared to be reading it to himself. Everyones expression was impassive, almost stony, except for the prisoner, who was crying and shouting for his mother. What was, if anything, more disturbing, was his constant shivering, bordering on the convulsive. Bertie noticed a heavy chair against the wall – he was a totally helpless observer, the most junior man present. The man was dragged to the chair, the two soldiers tied him securely to it. Realising his desperate situation, the man started begging for his life. The padre went up to the tied man and may have offered some words of comfort as he stuffed a black hood over his head... seconds later the padre raised his hand and moved well to the right, as did the two soldiers. The man was still struggling desperately but the heavy chair had hardly moved. The six soldiers had lined up with their rifles aimed towards the man.

"One of you has a blank round... aim...fire at my command." The officer had his arm up. The man was still screaming; it looked as if he might free one of his legs.

The officer lowered his arm. The shots rang out and the man was dead, although the officer walked over and shot him through the temple just to make sure. John motioned for them to move forward and he and Bertie carried the stretcher to the chair. The soldiers untied the man and laid him out. John covered him with a shroud and he and Bertie carried the body to the ambulance. "Just put him anywhere." The padre said, as he went inside "I have to deal with the living."

Just before they left, Bertie saw him join the soldiers for a hearty breakfast through the window. Your own living, he thought.

The officer was strolling by the ambulance having a smoke. Bertie just asked him "Why?"

"Oh, he did not go over the top yesterday. Court martial four o'clock, condemned twenty-five past. Sentence confirmed 10pm and now ..."

Bertie nodded - what was there to say?

"He was suffering from shell shock." John said after they had driven a short while. "You can cop it if it happens to you at the wrong moment."

"I can see that," said Bertie. "Where are we going to put him?"

"I know a place, he deserves some peace, please can you say a few words?" So they found a clearing in the wood and buried him with as much dignity as possible. Bertie did say a few words. They did not even know his name. They erected a rudimentary wooden cross and scratched 'To an Unknown Soldier'.

They were on duty in the trench again; there was no activity on the British side nor was any expected but there was a lot of German shelling. It stopped and Bertie gingerly looked down the mirror to see Germans advancing - equally brave men, he thought. None the less they are coming to try to kill us.

Led by a tall officer, gradually they were shot down one by one. The British did not have as many machine guns as the Germans. Instead there was accurate rifle fire. Bertie hated seeing the young men being slaughtered. There was no hatred in him. They had almost reached the British line when the defenders came over the top in a swift counter attack and the small German party was overwhelmed.

Immediately a ceasefire was signalled and they went forward to pick up the wounded: one of the other stretcher bearers called to Bertie: "This German is trying to say something; do you understand him?" Bertie went over, the proud uniform was muddied and the pickelhaube helmet lay in the dirt but his face was unmarked.

"Gunter." Bertie gasped "Gunter?"

The Lieutenant looked at him. "Herr Professor, is it you? The Englishman here is also wounded."

Bertie replied in German. "No, Gunter, I'm afraid you are more seriously wounded. I will try to get a message to your father, you must rest now." Gunter did relax.

And then to John. "He was trying to tell us to take the Englishman first." "Brave man," said John.

They were moving the new set of wounded to the ambulances waiting to go to the casualty clearing station. The sergeant stopped to take charge and sent Bertie back for another trip to the trenches. A ranging shell from the Germans landed very close to him. He thought he was flying as he was blown a long distance from the path. Bertie landed in a pool of thick mud which saved his life. Miraculously no shell splinter had touched him. He was breathing and completely knocked out but virtually invisible. There were no other casualties and no one else happened to have been near the explosion. It was only at the evening roll call it was noticed that Bertie was missing and it was too late to mount a proper search.

Bertie's letters were sometimes vague in detail and Joyce realised that there was censorship and that Bertie's position as an MP meant that he had to comply very strictly. But the letters still arrived every day, until one day there was nothing.

He was woken up by a dog licking his face. He instinctively realised that not only was it being friendly but trying to save his life. Then the cold hit him. He tried to get up but could only manage to crawl. After a few yards he had to stop. But he was out of the mud, if still drenched. He was gasping terribly and realised that his asthma had returned with a vengeance. He could not lie down. A star shell lit up the ghastly landscape. Bertie could now see his rescuer, a large Alsatian. She barked and Bertie saw a small pile of straw. He crawled on to it and fell into a deep sleep. He never saw the dog again.

The next day there was another big push and the unit were fully engaged. So it was two days later at first light, before John could organise a proper search and Bertie was soon found, drenched and speechless. John accompanied him to the casualty clearing station. Bertie was given a fresh, dry uniform but was way past their level of care. He was only intermittently conscious. John did not like the way he wheezed. He insisted he go to hospital and made it his turn to escort the ambulance train. He wrote a letter to Joyce telling her that at least Bertie was alive.

6 THE CORPORALS SUIT

Ambrose Woodall passed his exams with flying colours. Despite the war there were a lot of ceremonies and parties. Instinctively he was suspicious of these events because of his Primitive Methodist background but he did like the odd drink. He was always surprised how much alcohol loosened tongues. He realised that while God had given him a rare talent, to use it properly he must learn to fight his own corner. To get anywhere he needed to perform as well in social meetings as he had in the Examination Hall. He would have to overcome the class barriers to get the job interviews that would secure his future.

He was now over thirty and volunteered for the Royal Army Medical Corps. By this time, casualties were reaching London hospitals in large numbers so he was in no doubt what he might be up against. He made every effort to ensure his younger brother, Jimmy, persevered in his efforts to qualify as a surgeon.

No more white feathers, he thought. He had tried to explain his position to the ladies but they were not interested. It had hurt. But now he would be joining at a time of his own choosing. Of course he realised he was lucky and the vast majority of men did not have that luxury. He was also instinctively suspicious of politics and politicians. Although he recognised the basic justice of the original call to go to war, he could not believe how much it had now come to dominate daily life. So he could now start to gain the necessary experience to further his career, maybe just not quite in the way he had foreseen.

In the chest was a leather bound collection of letters written by Ambrose from the front to his mother in Marple.

After what seemed to him to be an inordinate amount of waiting around, he was sent to a base hospital at Etretat in France as a Captain. As a surgeon, he should have been a Major or

Colonel but this never happened. He had been used to the well ordered life of a leading London hospital. Now he would need all his social skills to survive. Etretat was led by people who often seemed to have little medical experience. Some were there just to avoid being in the trenches. The buildings were ramshackle and often dirty. But it was the scale of casualties passing through that really shook Ambrose. Sometimes whole trainloads would have to be processed. It was basically a huge triage operation. Some were sent straight back to Britain. Ambrose thought the hospital could treat far more casualties on site and reduce the stress of the journey. But many of the patients wanted to go home for any number of reasons. Some had a sheer terror of the Front and the trenches and there were some injuries that even on superficial inspection had been self-inflicted. On the other hand the Army wanted the troops to recover and many were sent back to the Front far too soon. Ambrose thought the Military, in the form of the Major in charge of the hospital, had too much power to influence what should have been medical decisions. In civilian life, if a patient was treated and recovered, they returned to their normal lives, miserable though these might be in some cases. Here Ambrose realised he was sending men to their deaths. Although he had not created the situation, he felt he could not entirely escape the responsibility. Despite all the complaints in his letters home, Ambrose did not look unhappy in the photos of him in front of the hospital.

A train had been diverted from the Somme because the local facilities had been overwhelmed. Ambrose was doing the basic assessment of the casualties on the train when he came across a Corporal stretcher bearer. He did not have any obvious physical wounds so he indicated that the corporal was to be taken off. The sergeant escorting the carriage came up to him and said in a quiet but firm voice: "This man has been through a lot, Sir. He was found lying in the mud after being missing for a couple of days. He could not speak and did not know where he was. He still doesn't have much idea now. I think he also suffered from asthma." said John, motioning towards Bertie's unconscious body.

"Friend of yours?" Said Ambrose.

"Yes Sir, I am proud to have known him."

"Well, he's not dead yet," said Ambrose as he examined the body more closely, taking temperature and pulse. "You are right, Sergeant. He's suffering from exposure and clearly not a young man. He needs much better care than we can provide. I think you may have saved your friends life." Bertie was sent home to London.

Ambrose was just beginning to find his feet and try to improve things when he was sent to No 70 Casualty Clearing Station much nearer the Front Line. 'Just to get me out of their hair', he thought. The Station was a tented affair where casualties were assessed and most were sent on to the base hospital. Sometimes Ambrose still had to perform life-changing operations with primitive operating facilities. However he had some reasonable digs in the adjoining village. Because the flow of casualties was very variable, sometimes the staff would relax in quiet times at a basic local bar. He was ordered to report to 23rd Division as battalion medical officer after a couple of weeks.

Alistair returned to Bertie's journal.

"So now I'm raising funds by lying in hospital," Bertie said to Emma.

"Yes, the War Office is funding your care."

"It's good to see our efforts went to such a good purpose… no seriously, I'm very grateful to be so close to you all."

When Joyce got the letter, Emma had immediately used some of her contacts to get Bertie to be moved to the Manor House Hospital.

Harried by the small group of Liberal rebels to spell out its war aims in terms that might form the basis for negotiation the government had been forced into a debate.

Bertie got up, put on his grubby uniform and managed to walk past the sleeping nurse at the desk and out of the hospital, undetected. He ordered a cab – the driver looked at him doubtfully. "I do have the fare." said Bertie "House of Commons please." Two armed guards stopped him at the entrance and still would not let him pass even though he showed them the Order paper. Not to be beaten, he went round the back and used his key as a Bar Committee member to open the door of the cellar. He stumbled over a barrel. The barman opened the trap door and saw the uniform. "Don't worry, I'm not Guy Fawkes." Bertie said as the barman helped him up.

"I think this calls for a drink, Sir," he said.

Bertie was sitting with his port when a well-known voice said. "Well you managed to get here at least, you haven't missed much. Mind if I join you. I think you need another one." It was Stanley Baldwin, now a junior conservative member of the coalition.

"Won't you get arrested for consorting with the enemy?"

"Look, I heard what happened. I may not agree with what you say but you do have the right to be heard. That's what this war is about, at least partly. Do you know what I'd do?"

"No idea." said Bertie.

"I'd go to my tailor and get him to make a suit with the features of a Corporal's uniform. There are no rules against that."

"I think that on this occasion, I am going to follow official advice." said Bertie. A week later the house cheered as he stood up in his new uniform and told the house that he had served a number of months as a Corporal. He was sure that almost all of the ordinary soldiers he had met were in favour of a negotiated honourable end to the war, preferably as soon as possible. It was the only time in the war that a corporal in uniform entered the chamber and it did have some impact. The Chancellor of the Exchequer, Bonar Law, was forced to reply, if not comply.

 Afterwards he was congratulated from all sides of the house, including the new Labour Leader, Ramsay Macdonald. Stanley invited him for another drink. "I will accept," said Bertie "but it'll have to be some other time. The hospital don't know I've gone." "AWOL, in fact." Stanley sighed.

He managed to creep back into the ward past the sleeping nurse yet again.

He was woken up by Joyce holding up a newspaper. She was absolutely livid. "Bertie, we try our best to make sure you recover and now you get up to your old tricks."

"I had to go," he said.

"One more stunt like this and you will be going all right!"

And there it was. The suit of the Corporals uniform lay neatly folded at the bottom of the chest.

.

7 THE POET AND THE POLITICIAN

Stuck in between two pages of Bertie's journal was a note of from Bertrand Russell dated June 1917 inviting him to meet at the club.

"Your note intrigued me," said Bertie as they sat down.

"Let me introduce you to a fine young man." Bertrand Russell replied. A tall slim Officer walked forward and shook Bertie's hand.

"Siegfried Sassoon. I have read about you," said the Officer.

"Oh dear, I get a very bad press these days."

"No, I'm interested in the fact that you joined up as a private."

"Yes, that's true, and I'm here to tell the tale - just."

"So did I," said the Officer.

"Not much fun, was it?" Mused Bertie.

Sassoon handed Bertie a typed piece of paper. It did not take long to read. He looked up. "Is this your work?" Bertie asked. Bertrand Russell was about to protest but Bertie raised his hand.

"I've had help in drafting it, but it is what I feel." Sassoon replied.

"I have read some of your poetry, I'm glad you express what you feel. I take it you are on leave now, are you going back to the front?"

" No, I'm going to send them this statement."

Bertie thought for a moment. "Oh, they'll love this. I have to say that if you were a private it would be immediate court martial. When I was a stretcher bearer, I buried the body of a man who refused to go over the top despite the fact he had obvious shell shock. He had a court martial lasting less than half an hour and was shot at dawn the next day."

Bertrand Russell looked absolutely appalled. "However, this could buy you some time. If, and I mean if, and I can't say when, I manage to read this in the House – I'm guessing that's why I'm here, there will be consequences, for me a little perhaps, I can live with that, that is my job, I even get paid to do it. But you have to realise what this could mean for you: this will change your whole life; there will be no going back. Are you sure you want to go through with this?"

Sassoon stood up with dignity. "I've said what I feel." He repeated. "I risk my life every day at the Front. It can't be worse than that." They shook hands.

Spontaneously Bertie said: "If you were my son, I would be very proud".

Alistair looked up the history. Some momentum for peace was building up. The German Reichstag passed its own peace proposal on 19th July 1917 and there was a House of Commons debate on 26th but the British government still refused to set out terms as a basis for negotiation and on the ground, or under it, gave its response to the peace moves in no uncertain terms. 19 out of the 23 huge underground mines blew up in the largest simultaneous underground explosion to date. 10,000 Germans were instantly entombed and British troops did make significant gains, if not a breakthrough.

As head of the local Casualty Clearing Station at Ouderdom, Ambrose started the longest shift in his career. For the next 30 hours he and his team dealt with over 1200 casualties, performing hundreds of operations.

On 21st July Bertie set a long stop by raising a straight Parliamentary Question to Ian Macpherson, the Under Secretary of State for War, enquiring whether any disciplinary action had been taken against Sassoon.

On the 23rd of July, bowing to Graves' insistence, he appeared before a Medical Board and was immediately sent up to Craiglockhart, a sanatorium for Officers near Edinburgh, having been assessed as suffering from neurasthenia, at the time the only diagnosis that avoided being shot as a deserter.

Meanwhile, perhaps because the government was more vulnerable than it appeared, soldiers in mufti were being increasingly used to break up peace demonstrations, including one in Glasgow. This sparked a House of Commons debate.

Bertie maintained there were as many soldiers who wanted peace by negotiation as there were against it and their right to be heard was being denied. Although Sassoon's case was slightly different and he would be accused of exploiting the young officer, Bertie realised that this debate gave him the golden opportunity to read out the statement in full. This might work, he thought, this might just work. But I will have to be good, really good. I need The Best. He went to Liberty's and got a new suit and top hat. It cost him more than he had earned in his entire recent military career but it was worth it.

Of course Sassoon himself was now being treated rather well by the authorities and probably would not relish the storm of abuse that a public reading would unleash. It was slightly disingenuous and the circumstances had changed but Sassoon had told Bertie not to withdraw the letter. As he himself had said, he had already gone over the parapet for real a number of times. Bertie thought of friends not so lucky and the wooden cross they had erected for the nameless soldier.

This was far more than the fate of one young man. It was a rare opportunity to speak for the millions who just wanted to get on with their lives and were never heard.

So in the middle of yet another apparently futile protest debate, Bertie, the tactical genius, seized his chance to read out the manifesto.

The manifesto had a very modern feel; was it really 100 years ago it had been read out? Alistair was immensely proud of his grandfather. It was a really brave speech. A great speech. Of course it did not materially change anything. The very next day thousands charged across the well-prepared killing fields of Passchendaele, as the 3rd battle of Ypres, erupted. Yet the speech is still remembered. Why? It was 3 years to the week since the original declaration of War. Bertie said Sassoon must have been one of the first thousand to join up. To go from that patriotic enthusiasm to the Soldiers Declaration reflected how completely the war had changed.

The Pals Battalions had gone over the top; men might still volunteer in 1917 but now they were outnumbered by conscripts. A different war altogether. A twentieth century war.

In the chest was the tattered typewritten manifesto.

I am making this statement as an act of wilful defiance of military authority, because I believe that the War is being deliberately prolonged by those who have the power to end it. I am a soldier, convinced that I am acting on behalf of soldiers. I believe that this War, upon which I entered as a war of defence and liberation, has now become a war of aggression and conquest. I believe that the purposes for which I and my fellows soldiers entered upon this War would have been so clearly stated as to have made it impossible to change them, and that, had this been done, the objects which actuated us would now be attained by negotiation. I have seen and endured the sufferings of the troops, and I can no longer be a party to prolonging those sufferings for ends which I believe to be evil and unjust. I am not protesting against the conduct of the War, but against the political errors and insincerities for which the fighting men are being sacrificed. On behalf of those who are suffering now, I make this protest against the deception which has been practised upon them; also I believe that it may help to destroy the callous complacence with which the majority of those at home regard the continuance of agonies which they do not share, and which they have not sufficient imagination to realise.

8 THE SIGNED PROGRAM

As the House rose, his close Liberal colleagues congratulated Bertie, even some opponents, some of whom had also fought in the trenches. It was time to accept that drink from Stanley. "The little Moltke strikes again! I cannot agree with you, of course. But I admire your spirit. You humiliated Ian, no bad thing from time to time. But it was your timing I really liked. Masterful. Pity we are on different sides. Somehow I think we're all going to hear a lot more about Siegfried Sassoon."

Bertie went home tired but elated, he had done his best. Joyce was asleep in the bed so he quietly joined her.

She took up the story.

When Bertie awoke the next morning, she was standing there with a copy of the Times. "Well, you've well and truly done it this time. The papers can't get at Sassoon so they're after you. I just can't go on as if nothing has happened when all our friends keep reading this sort of thing."

Just then the bell rang. "That's probably the Press now. I should have a large placard reading 'NO COMMENT'. Oh no, you stay there. You don't look at all well." It was true. Bertie stayed under the covers. He grew delusional, thinking if he made himself very small it would all go away.

It was the Trevelyans at the door. Charles had not been there for the speech but it was clear that Bertie had scored a major hit against the government, though at some cost, Mary noticed. She let Charles go upstairs to speak to the patient. "Get away from all this. Come up North."

" You sound like a Railway advert. Don't they read newspapers up in Northumberland?" Replied Bertie.

"Maybe they do, but I'm Lord Lieutenant, good as....and under the War Powers Act, I can lock them up... ravish their wives... whatever it takes."

"I'm not sure that's in the spirit of the Act."

"They make these unpopular speeches and then just retreat into the Club," said Mary downstairs.

"Or bed," said Joyce. "It does take it out of him. I do sometime wonder to what end."

"Perhaps it will be appreciated one day. Look there's a Commons recess soon. Why don't you two come up to Wallington with us while the dust settles."

"That is very generous. Are you sure?" Said Joyce. "It would be really good for us now."

"It is really beautiful up there, a different world. We'd love to show you round."

"We'd really like to come. Actually Bertie is still suffering some after-effects of his own War. I still don't really know what happened."

"It really will all settle, you know." Mary replied soothingly. The doctor diagnosed nervous strain. At least they're not going to send me to Craiglockhart, Bertie thought, I'm not an Officer. Complete rest was advised. Wallington beckoned.

No press cuttings from the aftermath of the speech had been kept in the chest, nor any of the predominantly hostile avalanche of letters.

She felt really happy when she and Bertie took a taxi with all their luggage, far more than Bertie had thought possible, to Kings Cross. The porters met them and they got into a 1st class carriage for the journey up to Newcastle. The train glided effortlessly through the British fog. It did not matter. They went into the

Pullman dining car for lunch near Grantham. The food was good and the wine excellent. Afterwards Bertie had a cigar, she a cigarette, in the smoking compartment. She looked across at the man who had been her husband for over two years; much older and very set in his ways, but she was comfortable in the relationship. How rude to think of him like an old slipper, she laughed to herself, yes, she loved him, she knew he loved her and would do for the rest of his life. The cigar had gone out and he was fast asleep as he often was in the afternoons. Late lectures, late night sittings, or just relaxed, it didn't matter, she let him be, he'd been through a lot, did not want to talk about it, though sometimes he shouted out in the night and woke up in a cold sweat. He always apologised but she knew he had seen things that no one ought ever to see. Oh dear, how morbid, no, she knew she could put the life back into him. She would never tell him, he must never know, she would be frivolous for him. How silly you are Joyce. Just then a beautiful rainbow appeared, she had not been aware of any rain but the brilliant colours seemed to signify a new start for her and for them. Let him sleep, he'll have some work to do in the evening.

Bertie described the same journey. He had been in a delicious snooze, he often slept on trains but he could not remember being so relaxed.

It seemed so long since he had taken a proper break. When he had become an MP, gosh that was seven years ago, he was straight into the Peoples Budget and then it just seemed one crisis after another. And that was before the war. It had become all encompassing, he had been lucky to survive but he had returned to the thick of it, the grim slog in Parliament trying to stop the war. In the midst of it all this girl, this young woman, had agreed to be his wife. She could not have made him happier. He looked across at her staring out of the window - what are you thinking?

"Are you happy my dear?" He asked gently.

She turned to him. "Yes, immensely." And she came across and kissed him on the forehead.

"I must have been asleep."

"I think you were, my dear." They both looked out of the window to enjoy the rainbow. Arriving at Newcastle a connecting train was waiting to take them to Morpeth where a large car awaited. Joyce could not believe the stunning countryside and the house with beautiful grounds. The room was very comfortable. She had a light wash and Bertie relaxed in the bath while Joyce prepared for their first evening. She felt like a debutante. Bertie had actually emerged from his bath and dressed for dinner looking very smooth. "May I escort you downstairs, madam?"

"You may sir; indeed you may." As Bertie walked down the large staircase with Joyce on his arm, he could not have felt prouder and she looked, well, absolutely stunning. This is going to be quite a fortnight, he thought.

Charles was able to spend most of the time with them although he was a different man up there, going hither and thither like some medieval prince patrolling the marches. I thought we were at war with the Germans, not the Scots, Bertie thought. Instead of an invasion they ventured over the border in a wholly peaceful way; Joyce really loved the wild landscape. Of course if you looked underneath the surface, all the villages were denuded of young men, off to war and young women gone to factories on the home front. But now Bertie just relaxed and took strength from the warmth of the sun.

After the holiday, Bertie was summoned to a constituency meeting in Northampton. On the train, he went to the bar to find Leo Chiozza Money, his parliamentary neighbour and now government minister for Shipping. Bertie congratulated Leo on his idea of convoys for the North Atlantic. "Well it has worked so far and given us a lifeline. Look Bertie, I know you are involved in that Charity Hospital."

"The Manor House?"

"Yes, that's the one. You do realise that after the war, the land will be sold to the highest bidder, hospital buildings or not."

"To be honest, I hadn't given it a second thought," replied Bertie.

Next morning he went to the meeting to decide which of the two sitting Liberal MPs would represent Northampton at the next election. Under the new Representation of the People Act, all constituencies would now have only one MP. Bertie thought he would lose because of his voting record against the government, but it was not by much.

Jessie Finch, the Chairman, gave him the offer of being a candidate at another seat. "This is not a bribe: it's thanks for being our MP for eight years."

Bertie looked taken aback. Jessie continued. "Good luck, whoever you fight for. I know you have your doubts."

"I'm not good at secrets."

"The world is changing Bertie, for all of us. The old Liberal party of grandees, it's over."

"Now it's architects like you, you mean." said Bertie.

"We have better plans!"

John Dyer's captain had bought him a pair of tickets for a show at the London Coliseum - it was the best night of John's life. He and his childhood sweetheart, Ethel, were part of an audience of nearly 4,000 people, watching George Robey – it was a charity event for the new Manor House Hospital and everybody joined in the spirit of the occasion. Robey held the audience in the palm of his hand as with the other he drew a cartoon on the stage and auctioned it for hundreds of pounds. When he announced the total raised so far, somebody made sure it reached another milestone. In the end the concert more than paid for all the hospital buildings. John successfully proposed to Ethel. Joyce and Bertie were also at the show.

Alistair picked up the programme signed by the great man. The hospital was officially opened soon afterwards.

Ambrose, now at 36 Casualty Clearing Station was dealing with the new casualties from Passchendale. In November 1917, he was posted to the Italian front, part of five divisions sent by Britain to shore up the situation after the disastrous allied defeat at the battle of Caporetto.

9 FIGHTING THE DON

Rumours from the Western Front began to circulate in the House.

Bertie had heard it all before. All over by Christmas. So long ago. But this time it was true. The truce was holding. No more fighting. It hardly seemed possible. Then he heard that Wilfred Owen had been killed six days before the Armistice. He had met him previously. Another fine young man. In yet another fruitless peace debate, Bertie had quoted from Anthem for Doomed Youth. And now the poet was gone. What could possible justify all this sacrifice?

Bertie's journal stopped abruptly. Alistair looked at Joyce's account.

Bertie had almost broken down completely. He wanted to step out of public life altogether and go back to finishing his book on the Indian Money Supply. Interesting though this might be, she pointed out, they would not be able to rely on her father's generosity indefinitely. Anyway he had to pull himself together because they had a wedding to go to.

Joyce was so happy as she and Bertie arrived at the church. Because he had been feeling so low, she was much more nervous this time than at their own wedding, this time it was Percy and Dorothy. He had been offered a lectureship in South Africa and they had to go there almost immediately, missing Christmas.

"Do they celebrate it over there?" Emma asked Dorothy, who was born in Basutoland.

"I think we have heard of it, my uncle used to put on his loincloth especially for the occasion." She said, standing up to Emma.

"I'm sorry, I didn't mean it that way – please remember us to your grandmother."

"You're right in one way, she is very frail and it really is a long journey."

"Well, I'm glad you've made it ....and your sister Mosa?"

"I'm not sure she can come; she is involved with refugees in Germany and the Balkans."

"Children, isn't it?"

"Yes their plight is terrible."

"At least she is trying to help."

"She and Eglantyne are setting up a new charity, Save the Children. You are still trying to keep the hospital going over here: it's the best legacy from the war – Mosa and I really loved working in Yvetot; it was the making of us."

"Well, I'm glad Percy went over there and met you but I'm not sure what is going to happen to the hospital; we have to bid for the land now the war is over."

"How ridiculous! I'm sure you will think of something – by the way; why have you ordered so much wine?"

"You obviously don't know the Holmans in action."

Lily came in dressed in black as usual. "I could use somebody like you at my new school in Kent." She said to Dorothy.

"Thanks for the offer but we're off to Cape Town."

Mosa hadn't made the service but half way through the reception she burst in with the Buxtons and Eglantine with the latest news from Germany. It was another good party hijacked.

"Dorothy has been upstaged by her sister yet again, she won't like that." said Percy to Bertie.

"Thank you for the offer of the house while you are away in South

Africa," he replied.

"I'm sure Joyce wanted North Square; many thanks for the reference by the way."

"The least I could do, I thought you should have got a first but did not tell you at the time; but we've all travelled a long way since then."

"It's Dorothy with the first," replied Percy.

Bertie now found himself a foot soldier in the epic political struggle of the giants of the next quarter century: Lloyd George, Stanley Baldwin, Ramsay Macdonald and eventually Winston Churchill.

The start was not auspicious. He arrived at the station in Sheffield. No one was there to meet him. He went to the Town hall and tried to pay his deposit. He was ushered into an office. There was a man behind a desk who paid him no heed. After a while Bertie coughed, he thought politely. The man glared and Bertie explained his business. The clerk looked at him as if the Don constituency was in a foreign country.

"Have you got the money?"

"Er, yes. Do I have to pay now? "

"Yes, if you want to be a candidate. And you have to get at least ten percent of the vote to get it back," said the clerk with relish.

He did seem particularly unpleasant. It was not a good omen, particularly as Bertie did not know a single voter.

I can ill afford to lose this now, he thought, especially as his father-in-law had given him the money for election expenses. He had not expected to have to blow it all immediately on the deposit. He walked down the street. This was a brand new seat and the official Liberal Party did not exist or rather it had been hijacked by the new National Democratic Party that crucially carried the Lloyd George Coupon. Bertie was the official Liberal candidate but in name only: he had no agent, no party organisation, no friends, and since paying his deposit, no money either.

Bertie had not wanted to involve Joyce at all at first but she knew he needed her, even before she got out of him what had happened, and more importantly what had not. "We'll have to fight for this, if you want it." She said.

"I thought I did but I do get so tired; sometimes I can't see the point."

"I know. Look. We'll have a go at this and then we will have a good break somewhere and decide what we want to do for the future. We do not have much time. There is one thing I can help you with...."

Under the new Act, the government had almost completely given in to suffragettes, giving all women over the age of 30 the vote in 1918. It would have been 21 there and then but for the fact female voters would have outnumbered the males immediately due to the War dead. Countess Markievicz was the first woman MP but did not take her seat as she represented Sinn Fein. It was Nancy Astor who was the first to sit in Parliament in 1919.

Joyce designed and wrote a page for the new voters. It was innovative and she had a flair for producing election material, a page in the manifesto for women's issues: she forced Bertie to hone his ideas down into clear simple statements. It was Joyce's first election and she impressed, getting stronger as the campaign progressed. Taking meetings on her own, she began to represent the new face of confident women with their own opinions, taking her share of hecklers naturally, one accusing her husband of being a pacifist. She immediately responded by saying that he was the only candidate who had actually served in the war. She found she liked the audiences and they liked her. She felt Bertie had stuck by what he believed in and that had left him with no party machine. Talking to voters, Joyce realised that although Bertie was better known than the other candidates, censorship had prevented some classic debates in Parliament during the war from being widely circulated; debates that might, just might, have saved millions of lives. Anyway that was then. What was to happen now? People wanted a future to believe in. As she listened to his speeches, Bertie was beginning to catch the public mood for change. She was not the only one to be mesmerised by his voice. You would not guess he was virtually on his own. She began to sense that the tide was turning in his favour. People had come to listen at meetings and some had been moved enough to offer their help and support. But there was not enough time. The vote was less than five weeks after Armistice Day and the count would not be until after Christmas.

"Win or Lose, let's go up north and have a ball in the New Year," said Charles Trevelyan. Mary thought it was a great idea to celebrate the end of hostilities and try to return to something like the spirit before the war.

Bertie had done much better than anyone had expected, including himself. But it was over. Nationally the Coupon candidates had won easily. The old Liberal Party was fatally split and the advanced wing decimated. Bertie did manage a reasonable speech at the count. They thanked their supporters warmly; they had worked their hearts out but for nothing, literally: defeat had been just 2000 votes, much less than he feared. At least Sidney would get his money back. But defeat it was; it may as well have been 20,000. Joyce and Bertie walked out, heads held high, with expressions of sympathy from all sides of the political spectrum. They walked slowly back to the hotel. It was very cold but neither of them felt it.

Joyce suggested they have a drink. This was the time to get drunk. Perhaps fortunately the bar was crowded and no one recognised them. In the morning they went happily down to a great breakfast. "I think we are done here," said Joyce. Bertie nodded. He paid the bill, they took a taxi to the station and were on their way north to the ball.

10 THE TOP HAT PLOT

Joyce was disappointed, of course. She looked across to Bertie. He would be really upset and hurt. But she must support him, to raise him to fight another day. Her blood was up. She felt they had nearly won. Next time... she knew there would be a next time... they would have much more time to prepare and win, together. Joyce loved him and realised what a great team they made.

Mary Trevelyan looked superb as did all the other ladies. Joyce loved being a part of it. As the butler invited the assembled company to take their partners, somehow the memories of the great Liberal Balls of the past were awakened, and the Grand Whig gatherings before that.

As then, the older men were in the smoking room, Charles ensconced in his favourite armchair with a large cigar. "So who would be a Liberal now?" Bertie said.

"Even if you had won, where would you be?" Charles asked.

"Probably sitting on my own in the House," Bertie conceded. "I'm surprised I did that well, and you only lost by 200 votes," he added, turning to Noel Buxton.

"You said you had something you wanted to tell us, Charles."

He had assumed what his friends called his conspiratorial look. "Well, as you know, I am friendly with Ramsay Macdonald and he has asked me to tell you that you are all welcome to join the Labour party."

"Free admission for the first year?" Asked Bertie.

"No, I don't just mean paying a small subscription and getting membership through the post – no, what Ramsay Mac wants you to consider is fighting the next election under the Labour flag. He thinks the party needs experienced MPs like you to make it plausible to the country, the city and, frankly, the establishment."

"Why can't he get people from the Welsh valleys or Red Clydeside; I'm not exactly cloth cap." Bertie asked.

"Oh they will in time but Ramsay Mac and Philip Snowdon think it will take a generation to establish what he calls a natural Labour government. In the meantime, established ex-Liberal MPs would provide a credible alternative right away. It's the Top Hats for now."

"I seem to remember we fought our parliamentary war under your banner in opposition to the government. We're not ministerial material. We're yesterday's men." said Bertie, not entirely believing it himself.

"But you could be so much more – we need your parliamentary tactical flair – we need everything we can get."

"Thanks a lot." said Noel "I guess there is nothing to lose. Anyway, we've all moved far too far to the left of the old support base."

"The Liberal party is doomed anyway because the split will never heal properly." Charles continued. "Think about it. Oh and to help you, we are offering winnable seats and if possible, good local agents to smooth your path and help you win and retain those seats."

"Don't the constituents get a say in this new Jerusalem?"

"Bertie, this is a serious offer."

"And I'll discuss it with Joyce."

"Don't be too long." Said Charles.

Although they certainly had not gone along with Bertie's increasingly left wing views, Sydney and Emma were sympathetic to Bertie joining the Labour Party. At least I won't have to lend him his deposit, thought Sydney. Anyway there was a more immediate problem. Bertie had no independent means and he was persuaded to go back to his old haunt of the London School of Economics.

Bertie got out of the taxi and cautiously walked into the building. He was surprised how little had changed. He felt a great sense of coming home. He had thought of it as a defeat, a retrograde step, but now it seemed right to resume a career in lecturing, if they would still have him. And they did. His record in parliament chimed exactly with the new mood in the School. And there were vacancies: sadly, colleagues had died or been killed but also there was a surge in demand from young men coming back from the war… and young women from the factories.

Early in the New Year he got up to begin his first lecture. The Hall was packed. He did not realise that Adam Smith had become so popular. Suddenly the students stood up, clapped and cheered. Bertie could not believe it.

After a minute, he raised his hand for quiet. "That was a short lecture." They laughed. "No thank you all. I hope you'll all be clapping at the end." And they did. He was enjoying being back.

Joyce and Bertie's son Patrick was born safely at the beginning of November. A week later Bertie stood outside Westminster Abbey and saw the wooden coffin of the Unknown Warrior being taken from the gun carriage. The wood was from Hampton Court estate and there was a medieval crusader's sword and an iron shield bearing the inscription 'A British Warrior who fell in the Great War 1914–1918 for King and Country'. How appropriate, Bertie felt but he could not stay there for long.

He found himself much closer to Joyce. She saw that his mind was getting much more alive after the experiences he had during the war, the long term effects were not recognised for many years. She had taken Charles Trevelyan's offer seriously. She had not forgotten the need for preparation. She encouraged him to use his time to study himself. He wrote a book on parliamentary procedure. And they joined the Labour Party. He was not alone. The popularity of the government began to wane as problems arose with the negotiations at Versailles and civil war erupted in Ireland. Above all perhaps, not enough homes were being built for the heroes and hundreds of thousands were thrown out of work as wartime government contracts dried up. It was so much harder to regain the pre-war markets for goods, especially coal.

Bertie found himself thrashing out new policies with the leading intellectuals of the Labour party and the Fabian Society, including Hugh Dalton and the Webbs. He felt they had arrived when he and Joyce were invited to a Socialist Weekend at the Webbs' house in Surrey.

They were both excited when they arrived in this Brave New World. They had both liked walking in the Surrey Hills, which had been one of their permitted activities during their chaperoned courtship.

Although game, even Aunt Lily had not always been able to keep up. The taxi had brought them from the station. Many had cycled but Bertie and Joyce had never taken to it. Anyway even the Webbs had servants. It would be very difficult to run any sort of House Party without them. However many of the guests were still uncomfortable. This is ridiculous, Bertie thought, worse than the LSE. He put up his hand and said. "Look it's a nice day, why don't we go for a walk." Everybody was so surprised and Beatrice Webb smiled at Bertie; they all shut up and the magic of the Surrey woods worked its charm. There was a much better humour when they returned. The debate lifted to discuss the imposition of a Capital Levy. This was narrowly carried. Bertie was quite impressed because a working party was appointed immediately to study the question. He volunteered and was accepted.

Joyce found the debates heavy going both in content and earnestness. Feigning a headache she slipped out in the afternoon and managed to get to her cousin's house in nearby

Peaslake, where she caught up with another cousin, the artist Duncan Grant. She managed to get back just in time for supper. She had missed the debate on whether contributions to National Insurance should be voluntary or compulsory.

Rather Dry, Alistair thought, I can't blame you, Grandma. Then he remembered she had told him that other cousins of hers had nearly divorced over the issue.

Other aspects of the weekend were less satisfactory. During the first afternoon tea, Joyce was asked by a well-known author whether she believed in Free Love. She said no and that was the end of the relationship. When Joyce told Bertie he laughed, which really annoyed her. "I was just thinking of all those Martians," he said.

"O you are so silly sometimes, Bertie."

The Webbs did not believe in sweated labour so refused to use coal. Unfortunately, there was no effective alternative so the house was freezing and Joyce and Bertie both went down with colds.

Such weekends were limited to the summer in the future, although they went to many others in warmer surroundings and Bertie gave lectures at WEA events.

Bertie got on the train for Keighley at Leeds Station. The ticket collector, Nigel Hawkins, recognised the passenger, who was deep into a book on economics. Well, you're in for a shock up here, Nigel thought. He interrupted Bertie politely to see his ticket. He smiled and presented his watch as surety. "My wife will pay at Keighley."

"No need for that, Sir. I'll take your word."

"I'm not good at faces but I do remember you now – it seems like decades ago."

"Good Lord, you're the stretcher bearer who rescued the German Officer."

"O Gunter, he'd been a student of mine before the war."

"Did he make it?"

"I think he's a banker in Frankfurt. I'm glad to see you've settled too."

"I can't complain. It wouldn't do much good, would it?"

Bertie's head was always in the clouds and he never carried any money around. Sometimes Joyce felt more like a valet than a wife but she always got him out of scrapes and became his self-styled political secretary. She did not really mind most of the time. It was certainly different.

A week before an invitation had arrived to go before a selection committee in Keighley. After some research into where it actually was, they both decided it was a good chance to stand for a winnable seat for Labour. And Bertie had served with the Pals. "Just be yourself." Joyce had said. "Let the voice do the talking." She had decided to come along in advance to see the lie if the land. It would be her fight too. It was a pleasant rail journey through country she had not seen before. Joyce wandered off from the station towards the centre of town. There was a Lyons corner house and she sat down at a table by the window. To her the High Street looked superficially like a smaller version of Sheffield, where they had been defeated nearly four years ago. It seemed a lot longer than that. She had urged him to fight on and this was their chance. There would not be many other opportunities, if any. Since the defeat they had established themselves in North Square. Somewhat to her surprise Bertie had proved a very good father and family man. She loved him but thought he was by nature an Edwardian gentleman who would happily spend his evenings in the Reform Club or the Athenaeum whilst he was not in the 'best club of all': the House of Commons. She was digressing. If he did get elected would the family survive?

Yes, she thought. Did she really want to go back to being the wife of an MP? More difficult to answer, but yes under her own terms and she was confident of that. She knew it would not be easy to get back into Parliament but she was a fighter and although she had come in late in the day she had not liked losing at all, Liberal or Labour. She had strong principles but stronger feelings of right and wrong. She knew that Bertie represented something special and together they could make it happen. She met Bertie at the station. While her husband looked at the newsstand, Joyce settled his debt with the ticket collector, who was certainly impressed by her. "Oh please do surprise him." Bertie heard as he walked back across the platform.

That evening Bertie went into the Labour Club. He was met by a smart young woman with an air of quiet efficiency. "'I'll take you to the Selection meeting upstairs."

She led the way and opened the door for Bertie and followed him and sat down at the back of the room. The chairman rose up to greet him. It was the ticket collector. "Do I still owe you something?" said Bertie and the ice was broken.

Nigel looked round the room. There was a row of nods and a show of hands; nem con. "We'd love to have you as MP." Said Nigel, offering Bertie his hand. "And my wife, Claire, can be your agent." She stood up at the back and smiled at Bertie.

"Before I accept, there's one other vote, I need."

"I'm sure she'll accept."

"I never take my wife's opinion for granted."

Joyce thought he would be selected. Of course they had discussed the possibility, but this was real. Over a celebratory drink, he asked her opinion, looking her in the eye. "I can still decline. I did tell them that you had a veto."

"That would not have impressed them from what I gather."

"'No, there are women voters too, finding their feet. Even on the selection committee. Even my agent."

"Well, you've got my vote; but you knew that already." There was a pause. "Yes, of course I want you to be MP but..." He looked up at her. "But you will have to let me help you. I mean help you in my own way. I think you have a chance but it requires total effort and commitment from both of us. There will be problems. You know how we have lost friends because you have turned your back on the Liberal Party. The average Liberal will hate you. You and I will have to deal with this head on if you are to get in. Don't forget this has never been a Labour seat. If David Lloyd George decides to come here all bets are off. You are a pretty good speaker but he could swing this constituency with one speech." "'You're right, of course. Luckily for us perhaps, he is far too involved with affairs in London."

"Yes, affairs is right from what I hear."

"I don't think he realises how much danger he is in both from his Conservative coalition partners and in the country. In other circumstances I'd be an admirer but I feel he has gone too far to pull the Liberal Party back from oblivion. Anyway, they'd love to meet you."

"I've met the chairman already."

"So you did. That was a great start!"

So the next morning they went and met Claire and other party members. Joyce remembered the Liberal committee in Northampton but this was very different. For a start it took time to get used to the Yorkshire accent. And it was all too easy to sound patronising if you took your time talking. Joyce instinctively spoke as clearly and distinctly as Bertie had and this seemed to work well. Like Bertie she was a good listener and soon was getting a feel for what concerned the prospective voters. And female voters. As well as unemployment and housing, Joyce picked up their concerns about their children fighting another war. She began to have a good feeling about the place.

That afternoon they took the train to Howarth and walked up the steep street to the church. The shops were just closing but people were still hurrying about in the gaslight. The flagstones through the trees and large gravestones to the parsonage were dimly lit but they went past the church to get the last view of the moors as the light from the sunset before it was extinguished. This was part of the constituency as well as the mills in the valley. There was a strange eerie light that seemed to emanate from the moor and Bertie felt humbled as he realised he had a chance to right some of the injustice that had been denied many of the spirits that had joined Heathcliffe over the years.. They stood there until they got cold and turned round into the darkness of the graveyard.

It had been a long journey to get here but this is the place to represent, Joyce thought.

So began an unlikely but sustained love affair between the Keighley voters and the Lees-Smiths.

11 THE INDULGENCE

Ambrose stayed at his post in Italy well into 1919. He had made friends with a fellow Officer who was a sincere Catholic; he arrived at Ambrose' digs one morning. "We are off to Rome, I've arranged it all."

They had a brief tour of the Forum and some ruins, ending in the Vatican City. His friend left him in a cafe and went off. Ambrose wondered whether he had gone to pray.

"Come quickly," he said as he returned. They went up several dark alleys, through a door, down some passages, then into a chamber full of priests in all sorts of vestments. It was like a medieval court, even the Swiss guards were dressed in ancient uniforms. At the end of the hall there was an old man seated on a simple throne: his friend pulled him towards the frail old priest, his face almost parchment but eyes very alive and penetrating. Ambrose, despite his primitive Methodist hatred of outward show, was strongly drawn to the right hand, offered his in greeting. On the finger was a huge ruby ring, which seemed to mesmerise. Even Ambrose could not help believing that it went all the way back to St Peter. His friend had knelt in supplication but Ambrose grabbed the hand and kissed the ring. He looked the man in the eye and they held each other's gaze for a few seconds – the old man pressed a piece of paper into his hand and it was time to leave Benedict XV.

They were soon back in the thick of things but Ambrose felt strangely refreshed and this feeling returned from time to time for the rest of his life. He never told his mother of the meeting.

The piece of paper was in Italian. Ambrose had it translated: it was an Indulgence, a great grandchild of those that had paid for the building of St Peters. And there it lay in the chest. Alistair wondered whether it was transferable.

The Industrial Orthopaedic Society was set up as a new charity to rent out the Manor House Hospital site that had been purchased from the government by Carr and Younger.

Most of its current income was still for the care of wounded soldiers paid for by the Ministry of Pensions. But this began to decrease as the soldiers were discharged. The charity would devote itself to industrial casualties in peacetime.

Unfortunately things were not going so well on the ground. After the war Dudley had left the Manor House hospital to go abroad. He was replaced by a registrar, Victor Newland. As a temporary measure Victor and Sullivan, the hospital Secretary, lived in the nursing home in North End Road. Victor complained to the Executive Committee about Sullivan's inappropriate behaviour with another resident. However it was Victor who was forced to leave with a month's salary. His dismissal brought more resignations and a letter of protest to the Lancet, all of which naturally raised a lot of disquiet among the contributors.

During the turmoil, Sullivan appointed the recently discharged Ambrose as Resident Surgical Officer and his brother Jimmy as a registrar. Ambrose thought the post would tide him over while he considered his next career move. He could also keep an eye on Jimmy, the JW who wrote the manuscript history of the hospital. Ambrose moved into some very modest accommodation of a small sitting room in the Manor House and a bedroom shared with rodents scratching behind the skirting. Not so far from the Western Front, he thought, but quieter with better food. Somehow he felt at home.

It did not take him long to realise he was in the middle of a storm of intrigue. Members on the Executive Committee were openly trying ro render it bankrupt so that the Metropolitan Hospital could pick up its assets on the cheap. They had, therefore, stopped accepting money from the Ministry of Pensions.

After the scandal arose, Sister Mcglashan took it upon herself to monitor night-time events in the nursing home. There was a small recess in the main corridor into which she could squeeze unseen and be able to observe comings and goings. As she suspected, she did not have to wait long before she heard the unmistakable shambling steps of hospital secretary Sullivan coming towards her. As he passed she noticed in the dim light he was carrying a large bundle of banknotes. She could either grab the package, but then do what? He could just as well accuse her of theft. No, she had to wait. She let him enter the room of nurse Wade – ah, it's you, she thought, we'll see about that. He came out after a while, business completed. As she let him pass again she noted there was nothing in his hand or pocket, as she suspected there wouldn't be. He would be planning to elope with his lover. She opened the door of nurse Wade's room and turned on the light, more confident of controlling the situation by startling the astonished nurse. On threat of instant dismissal without a reference, even a possible criminal charge, nurse Wade had to cooperate. The money was handed over and she was told to keep silent, and particularly not to tell Sullivan what had happened. If they did elope it would have to be under their own steam. Although new, Ambrose seemed honest and unbiased. She knocked gently on his door – he was surprised to see her as he was not on-call. She showed him the money and explained how she had come by it. They counted it out; £1,500. "That would have done for us." Ambrose said; the financial situation was pretty shaky to begin with, even without this theft. Sullivan would have to go, of course.

"I'll need you to do me a favour." Ambrose said. He called an emergency board meeting. Bertie and Joyce were present. Ambrose had let Sullivan think that it was yet another doctor being difficult but then Ambrose demanded to know what was the latest financial position and why he had abrogated the Ministry contract. While Sullivan was prevaricating, there was a knock on the door and Sister Mcglashan came in with the notes and put them on the table. "Would this help?" She said sweetly and walked out.

Sullivan recognised the game was up. "We would have been much better off with the Metropolitan," he said "Police more like, if you don't resign now and go." Ambrose said and that was the last they saw of Sullivan. Nurse Wade had also applied for indefinite leave to look after an elderly relative who had become ill unexpectedly.

"Well, that was exciting." said Bertie. "Ambrose is quite a find." "Oh, I'm pregnant, by the way," said Joyce casually. Bertie was overwhelmed and Joyce had to put her arms around him. "It's alright, Dear. It happens all the time."

Ambrose and the new hospital secretary began to pull things around by managing to restore the contract with the Ministry of Pensions to give them the breathing space to forge an alliance with the Trade Unions. Starting with the London Busman, Ambrose persuaded them to contribute their pennies to become members of the Manor House Hospital, which began to build a reputation both for treating Industrial injuries and rehabilitating orthopaedic patients. Ambrose began to take on medical compensation cases on behalf of the Unions, starting with the National Union of Railwaymen. General Secretaries began to take notice as the NUR began to win big cases against the formidable legal teams fielded by the great railway companies and soon there were successful claims against employers in a wide range of industries, with Ambrose as the expert medical witness. The hospital began to steadily widen the trade union subscription base.

Nobody expected the Strike to happen. Ambrose had treated Arthur Cook, the miners' leader as a patient. He had been polite and courteous. Stanley Baldwin would pull off a last minute compromise. Tea and sandwiches at No 10, he was good at that; nobody better. So Ambrose went to a compensation case in Glasgow and was forced to stay for a fortnight. Sometimes the telephones worked but he feared others were listening; there were no newspapers. He refused to listen to State Radio and had no idea what was happening in the rest of the country. He thought the strike was ill-advised and was not surprised It officially ended after nine days.

Things looked different from his hotel window overlooking George Square. At one end was Glasgow City Hall, defended by soldiers, bayonets fixed; in front of them a troop of mounted police; a row of military ambulances stood menacingly at the side. A crowd of angry workers was marching up West George Street, steadily pushing several lines of police back towards the square. The atmosphere was incredibly tense; Ambrose felt the slightest spark could set off a massacre. He checked his medical bag and hoped this scene was not being repeated all over the country. The police lines were just holding. Just then a large car with a Red Cross pennant drove into the Square … Ambrose guessed a doctor. There was a very striking young woman sitting next to him. As the car drew closer he could see the grim mood on both their faces. When the car was level he could see she was heavily pregnant. Mistaking what was happening, the mood changed, stones were thrown, one hitting the car. Ambrose sensed the determination as the driver dodged the missiles and headed straight towards the crowd. At the last minute the police line rallied, forced back the rioters and cleared a way through. The car sped on its way.

12 THE ROLLS ROYCE AND THE CHARABANCS

Joyce's second pregnancy was more difficult and she was advised to go into hospital.

This would almost be the first child to be born in the Manor House. Realising there might be problems they were very keen to make it go as well as possible. In addition to the front line team, Ambrose, their rising star, was held in reserve in case things went badly wrong. He had very limited experience in this area but was a brilliant surgeon. It was a long labour, not helped by the midwife droning on interminably about her pension plans. As Ambrose stayed close by, he marvelled at Joyce's stoic resilience through the birth of twins. The first was a healthy boy, Christopher John, CJ almost from birth. His sister Isobel never thrived. Despite the desperate efforts of her exhausted mother, grandmother and sisters and the devoted nursing staff, a week later Isobel died.

Alistair had no idea of her existence.

She was laid to rest in a very private funeral. The family closed ranks to look after the remaining children. Three months later Sidney Holman also died suddenly, he was only 58; Emma was devastated. Percy and Dorothy returned from South Africa for the funeral. He was now head of the family and had to take some radical decisions. Sidney had moved into property and all of his houses were divided amongst the family – Joyce got Coryngham Road but it was agreed they would continue to rent the North Square house they were living in. The family paper business would probably have to be sold. "Where would you like to live? " Dorothy asked Percy.

"I now feel I have to be here in London."

"Well, why not?".

"I haven't got a job here for a start." Percy replied.

"But you do have a business."

"Yes, but I know nothing about it." He added almost to himself. "But Williams, the chief clerk of many years, does."

"Well why don't you have a chat and go 50-50?"

This enabled Percy to pursue his political interests as well; over the next 20 years he fought Twickenham unsuccessfully for Labour. Holman and Williams prospered, as it still does.

Unfortunately all this happened with some acrimony and resort to lawyers – Percy and his sisters were all strong minded in their own way and Emma was too devastated to mediate. The family wounds never really healed.

Joyce went North with Bertie for his first public meeting in the constituency. There was an air of expectation; Bertie came with some reputation. He had spoken up against the war but had also served in it. By now the fruits of victory, if any, seemed meagre indeed. Bertie criticised the harsh terms of the Versailles Treaty, supported Russia and Soviet workers and gave a clear exposition of party policy. His voice held the large hall, even if the audience did not agree with everything he said.

In the chest was the beautifully produced four page manifesto. The first page pictured an avuncular Bertie in wing collar and he invited the voter to consider his policies on pages two and three, whilst on page four, there was a letter from Joyce addressed to the women voters along with a studio picture of her with baby Patrick.

As the campaign progressed it became obvious that a strong bond was developing with the voters and the Keighley Times was increasingly sympathetic. There were enthusiastic local party workers with good trade union links. It all came together and Bertie won by 5000 votes in 1922.

There was a framed photo of a smiling Siegfried Sassoon and Wilfred Owen. This was always on his desk in the House of Commons.

It did not stay there long. Stanley Baldwin made a rare political error and called an election a year later. He lost his overall majority but Bertie lost in Keighley by only 500 votes. It cost Bertie his chance of joining his friends Charles Trevelyan and Neil Buxton in the first Labour minority government of 1924. The Top Hat plot was beginning to work.

Bertie went back to the LSE but there was another election in 1924 as the Liberals withdrew their support.

Neatly stored in the chest was a brilliant election poster. In a studio picture of Patrick and CJ now aged five and three, both with broad smiles, sat on a stool together. Probably a rare event but underneath was the legend: 'Vote for Daddy'. The family were really putting everything into regaining the seat.

However Bertie's journal took up the story.

"Have you read this?" said Joyce, presenting Bertie with a copy of the Daily Mail a week before the election. As he read through the letter he thought it might be a hoax, but if so it was very convincing. Gregory Zinoviev was a member of the Soviet Politbureau and had written a fraternal letter to the Labour party...supposedly. Electoral dynamite – if true… and devastating. It was denied, of course, but the press had a field day. Bertie thought the Labour party was doomed and they did lose 40 seats, but he won back Keighley and returned to the House of Commons. It had been the Liberals that had been the big losers. They had just 40 seats left with Labour now 151, but both dwarfed by Conservatives with 412. The letter is still a mystery.

There was a picture of a crowd of people standing next to two charabancs incongruously parked next to a Rolls Royce. But this was no ordinary holiday.

By 1927 most of the work had been done to rebury the dead on the Western Front into the marble graveyards and memorials. A trip was arranged for veterans from the Keighley Pals and relatives of the dead to see where they fell. They came from the whole social spectrum from the Captain, the eldest son of the mill owner Lord Redbroke, to his batman who had tried to rescue him. Both had been killed before they could make it back. Neither had been found. The Captain's father could not bear to go but his mother Edith went in the family Rolls Royce. The family made sure that everybody who wanted to go could do so, irrespective of means. Several charabancs were laid on and Bertie was invited. It was no secret he had served beside the Pals.

Most of the casualties had occurred on the 1st July 1916, when the Pals had gone over the top. Bertie knew that he would not have survived if he had still been there on that day. He had come by train from London and the party were standing by the trench from which he had gone out to pick up the casualties. He wished John Dyer was here. It was now covered in grass but parts were recognisable. Someone's boot still lay ten yards towards the German lines. They were not far away but it was dangerous to walk across to them with the barbed wire and unexploded shells that were still buried. Nobody wanted to; it was too painful. He found himself standing to attention as someone played the Last Post.

He heard the Rolls Royce pull up a few yards away. The chauffeur opened the door and Edith got out. She walked towards the trench. She looked across the wasteland where her son still lay. She just broke down and cried. It began to rain gently. In the mist over what had been the German lines, Bertie fancied he could make out two lonely figures, still standing to attention. He shook himself and escorted Edith back to the car.

The group were having supper together at a cafe in Arras that night, laid on by the Mayor.

"I'm not good at faces but I do remember you now – it seems like decades ago." said the Sergeant of the Pals to Bertie.

"You're telling me; I'm very glad to meet you again. Do you mind me asking you something? You don't have to tell me if you don't want to."

"Well, what do you want to know?"

"Do you remember a man being shot for refusing to go over the top?" The Sergeant thought or a long moment "How could I forget? How do you know about it?"

"I had to bury him; they wouldn't even tell me his name." The Sergeant told the story.

"I was about to go over the top and I found Colin; Colin Smith, was his name, cowering in one of the caves. I could see how far gone he was and I was just trying to hide him when an arrogant staff officer came round the corner at the wrong time. We hardly ever saw them, and certainly not in the trench, but there he was – he immediately saw what was happening and put the man on a charge. We never saw him again, but there was a postscript. Not long after Colin had been taken away, the Colonel came back from the attack, absolutely covered in mud and worse. He rapidly realised what had happened. I was standing behind him. The Staff Officer was still standing there looking pristine. "He had refused to go over the top, Sir." He said in a matter of fact way as if he had failed to polish his boots on parade.

"Haven't you heard of shell shock? This man was a casualty in need of treatment, nothing more."

"It's too late for that now, Sir." Said the Staff Officer smugly.

"Yes, I'm sure it is." said the Colonel. "What happens if I order you over the top, right now. It's light. They'll still be able to see that nice shiny uniform of yours." He went to wipe his muddy arm across the Staff Officer's face.

The man cowed. "There's the ladder. Up you go." The man hesitated. "Oh, disobeying an order on the field of battle. Or just another useless sacrifice. I think we all know a thing or two about that." the Colonel said, turning back to us survivors. The Staff Officer collapsed, sick with fear. "Oh get up, man." When he had composed himself, the Colonel went on. "The system will have to take its course now.; you're right about that. But if anything happens to this man, he will be listed as dying bravely in action, nothing else. Do I make myself clear? Otherwise I will have you transferred here in time for the next Big Push. And I'll be right behind you when you go over the top." He looked around at me. "This goes no further, Sergeant."

"Agreed Sir."

"And it never has. His parents have been spared the shame."

"And they still will be, rest assured," said Bertie.

"Where did you bury him?" asked the Sergeant. "The padre preferred a good breakfast to giving him any sort of funeral so we found a quiet spot in the wood and buried him there - I did say a few words."

"And he had a cross?"

"We had to put 'To an Unknown Soldier' on it."

"That was right." Said the Sergeant thoughtfully.

13 THE RED DISPATCH BOX

The family went all out for the 1929 election. This was obvious from the journals. Another proud family portrait stared out of the manifesto. An eight year old CJ stood up on a car bonnet at an outdoor meeting in a crowded square and urged the crowd to 'Vote for Daddy'.

On election night, Joyce was doubtful but as the piles of votes for each candidate began to mount, Bertie's confidence grew; he was right, he was back in. He thanked the voters and his party workers, who once again had given their all. He was just leaving when Claire came across to him and handed him a slim parcel. "We were going to give you this anyway, whether you got in or not – we've all collected for it." He opened it; inside there was a silver paper knife, inscribed with his name and Keighley. He was incredibly grateful, knowing how poor most of them were. "I can't accept this."

"Oh yes you can, you will be opening more important letters now."

He returned to London – there had nearly been a straight Labour victory – the first ever, enough to form a government. Nobody had said anything but there was an air of expectation. The next day an official letter arrived – it had one of those old British Exhibition stamps – they must have produced millions of these, he thought. He took his new paper knife and opened the envelope. It was an invitation to be Postmaster General; he was rather nonplussed; then he realised it was a Cabinet post. He went through to Joyce. "You've bloody well earned it," she said and hugged him.

"No." He said quietly. "We've earned it...I would be nowhere without you. Probably just marking exam papers in some academic backwater. Let's go out and enjoy it."

Alistair put the journal down. How right you were, Grandfather. Joyce had the organisational flair. Without her there would be no second political career with the Labour party. It was much more than that. Although Alistair was writing the story, grandmother had been here before. It wasn't random. She had been the one to decide what was in the chest; what would be seen and what was left out. Alistair was glad he was the one to open it. And there was the silver paper knife.

Bertie went into the ornate headquarters the next morning and it was soon clear just how big the Post Office was; it employed 250,000 people, probably the biggest single employer in the country. It had a massive programme for extending the telephone into rural areas and establishing international phone links with America and beyond. Just as he was settling into his new role he attended the first meeting of the new House of Commons. It was a strange feeling to take his place on the government front bench; It's nearly 20 years since I first came here, he thought, and he remembered trying, unsuccessfully, to catch the speakers eye for the first time. There had been hundred of duels since then, won and lost.

Stanley Baldwin stood up for the opposition to congratulate the new government. He said something about a new era in politics and caught Bertie's eye. He was no longer a foot soldier. The PM rose to reply for the government, not that new, he thought, nearly one-third of the cabinet had been Liberal MPs like himself, and a lot more had been in the minority labour government of 1924. The Top Hat plot had come to pass.

On the following Thursday there was an invitation to attend his first Cabinet meeting. Joyce fussed over him, making him look as tidy as she could and put him in a cab "You are NOT going on the tube today." She insisted. He sat back in the cab and relaxed – he could not believe the number of postmen he saw – poor sods, he thought, little do they know who's in charge. The cab stopped outside number 10; he gave the driver the fare and a tip.

"Good luck, Sir." He said.

"I'll need it." said Bertie, enjoying the moment as he stepped out.

There was a flash as a press cameraman caught him and Bertie turned and smiled broadly for a full photo – he had arrived. *And there was the Evening Standard photo.*

One day in cabinet, Ramsay Macdonald said. "Bertie has an announcement to make".

Bertie stood up; "The PM and I are going to accept the first telephone call from Australia tomorrow morning." There was muted applause. "And to celebrate I have a surprise." He clapped his hands and in walked a young CJ with a tea trolley and some homemade cakes.

John Dyer had risen steadily in the Post Office to become head of Barnes sorting office. He made sure Bertie and Joyce had no idea who would be welcoming them on an official visit. As soon as Bertie saw John, they just hugged each other as they both almost broke down. Spontaneously the crowd clapped and the pair bowed. *Another great photo.*

"We all thought he was there for the publicity. John said.

"Oh he's good at that." said Joyce.

"Well this time you would be wrong, he was a very brave soldier. I was proud to serve with him."

"Talking about me behind my back?" said Bertie

"Actually John was being very complimentary." said Joyce.

"It's still Bertie, and I would still be in France if it wasn't for you."

"Think nothing of it – you should thank the doctor, Captain Woodall; he was the one who diagnosed you with hypothermia and sent you home."

"Ambrose Woodall?"

"Oh yes, that's the man." Just as the visit was coming to an end,

John said.

"I'd like to invite you to Bethnal Green. I'm chairman of the local Labour party."

"Please chat to my Social Secretary."

"You never could organise yourself!" John said. Joyce nodded and they all laughed and made a date.

After the next hospital board meeting, Bertie went to search out Ambrose to thank him. He was directed down a long corridor, up some narrow stairs and down again and then found a door with Woodall on it. He knocked. "Come in."

Bertie entered a small room with a bed down one side of the wall and a single chair standing on the threadbare rug. "Is this all they've given you to live in?" Ambrose nodded.

"You're not exactly the cleaner here."

"You'd be surprised. Oh I don't really mind." he said, but Bertie did detect a little resentment.

"I've thought about asking for some land and building a house at my expense." Ambrose went on.

"I can see you've thought about it, I'm not surprised; there's not even a proper window; this is not acceptable. Jimmy and I will see what we can do."

. . . .

"You're a big employer now, Bertie," said Nigel, now the Regional Secretary of the NUR.

"I suppose I am." It did not seem like that. "How would you like to be sponsored by us." "Does that mean you would not check my ticket again?"

"No, I'd still do that. You would join us negotiating with the Big

Four railway companies."

So in time, Nigel and Bertie successfully won paid holidays and the right to have a friend or shop steward to be present at disciplinary proceedings. Bertie was invited to cross the Atlantic on the first cable-laying ship to New York. It was the best holiday Patrick and CJ ever had and the closest they got to their father.

Bertie became Education minister in a Cabinet re-shuffle. He missed PMG, at which he had really excelled, but at least he was still in the game.

"So they've chosen you to bury my Education Bill; et tu, Brute." Charles Trevelyan said.

"Actually, it's Bertie, I'll try my best but there are the cuts and religious opposition, a powerful brew."

"I suppose so; good luck anyway; we've come a long way, you and I." "And we still will," said Bertie, realising that probably would not be the case. The Education Act was passed and the ladder of opportunity widened slightly. He was also sworn in as a member of the Privy Council, I really have arrived now, he thought as he went through the gates of Buckingham Palace.

Vivian Hancock, headmistress of Greenways School said to her friend. "I know you are not interested in anything other than cricket but Bertie Lees-Smith has become minister of Education."

Siegfried Sassoon looked bored and sighed. "I obviously did him a great favour."

"You are so arrogant," replied Vivian. "Well, he's coming here."

"What, why here?"

"Well, he is the minister, and that is the sort of thing they do; visit schools. Why don't you come to meet him?"

"He won't remember me."

"Oh, I'm sure he will."

As the boys stopped clapping in the crowded hall, Bertie thought he saw a familiar face at the back of the audience. It can't be, he thought. But it was and they went out for a drink.

"Glad to see you've settled all right," said Bertie, looking at Vivian.

" O no, we're not together." Siegfried Sassoon replied.

"I saw you were talking to the German ambassador," said Joyce, who liked official visits. This had the desired effect of bringing Siegfried Sassoon down a peg. "Oh you were at the ball too."

"Yes, you wouldn't dance."

"That figures." said Vivian.

Bertie got up and fetched another round of drinks.

"Anyway, It's you I have to thank you for all those letters I got when the manifesto was reported in the press," said Sassoon.

Bertie replied. "Not popular, were we. I got my fair share of brickbats. Well in retrospect, I suppose it did us both good, I think some of my immunity rubbed on to you along with the help of your young friend, Robert Graves."

"Well I wasn't shot and I'm here to tell the tale, so I suppose I should be thanking you," replied Sassoon.

"And then there was Wilfred Owen." They were both silent.

"I have brought a peace offering." Continued Bertie after a while, handing him a ticket for the third test at Headingly. Donald Bradman will be there." Sassoon looked at it in amazement. "How on earth did you get hold of one of these? They are gold dust. "

"I suppose I'm Minister of Sport as well."

Sassoon paused and passed him a handwritten poem.

He fumbled for his glasses. "I must have left them at the school."

"O you are hopeless," said Joyce, taking the piece of paper.

"This is you." She said slowly. "You have been remembered."

It was a normal Thursday cabinet meeting but there was tension round the table before it even started. There were always rumours about how bad things were, especially in the last few days, but now they just might be true, thought Bertie. Ramsay Macdonald and Philip Snowden came into the room and there was a hush. The Prime Minister opened the meeting. "I think we had better get straight to it, gentlemen, I'll hand over to Philip." The Chancellor rose and outlined the stark options facing the government as they had to respond to yet another crisis to remain on the gold standard. "If we just leave, we will be accused of economic incompetence and there won't be another Labour government for a generation. Therefore we have to make deep cuts both in defence...." he paused "and unemployment benefit." This was too much for Bertie and six others. They voted against the cuts; the cabinet was split so the government resigned immediately. The King persuaded Ramsay Macdonald to stay on as Prime Minister so he formed a National Government with Stanley Baldwin and the Conservatives, who greatly outnumbered the few Labour and Liberal MPs who had stayed with Macdonald. When they went to the country for a mandate they were massively successful. The labour party only won 52 seats. Hundreds of their MPs were out of a job, including Bertie; there was no safety net in those days. Well at least he had been a General, he thought, of sorts.

His successor as Postmaster General had been Clement Atlee. He scraped in at Poplar by 428 votes and went on to lead the Labour Party in 1935. There was a nice Punch Cartoon with Bertie on an old fashioned two piece telephone. He got to keep the red leather ministerial dispatch box, inscribed H B LEES-SMITH Postmaster General. In a pocket inside was the neatly folded poem.

14 THE VISITORS BOOK

Ambrose nearly fell over a screen as he was taking the pulse of the formidable Ernie Bevin, general secretary of the Transport and General. It was fine and the patient appeared to be dozing peacefully. He was just about to go to the next bed when a voice boomed: "Good trip, Ambrose. Don't think you're going to get away that easily."

"And here was I thinking we had a satisfied customer," replied Ambrose.

"A sleeping one, you mean. At least I'm doing better than Arthur Cook." "We were all sorry he did not make it," said Ambrose.

"That wasn't your fault. There were many that did not mourn his passing. I never agreed with how he led the miners, but I did respect him. Anyway the staff look after me very well here and I am very grateful. When I have been awake, I have been observing things; you are getting pretty popular."

"We could do with a new wing," said Ambrose.

"Just what I was thinking," replied Ernie. So he arranged for the Union to give the hospital a loan to cover building a new wing of 50 beds.

Ramsey Macdonald was looking at a list of people to recommend for honours; he was learning how to use them for patronage; then he saw Ambrose Woodall on the list. At last, somebody to reward who actually deserved it.

In the chest there was a thick leather-bound book filled with letters of congratulation. Some famous names; shop steward committees from around the country; unions, long since merged and forgotten, but most from ordinary members of the public, all recognising Ambrose's achievement rising from a very humble position. The book was very moving to read.

Ambrose had the flu so he was forced to stay in bed for a week – in the tiny bedroom. This focused minds and the committee decided to build a residence appropriate for the chief surgeon, let alone a baronet. Bertie managed to commission Jessie Finch, his architect friend and ex-Liberal chairman from Northampton, to submit plans. He toured the neighbourhood to decide what was in keeping with the Hampstead locality and submitted outlines of two houses, one big, one small. The committee was going to opt for the small house; however Bertie and Jimmy suggested that a small house would be dwarfed by the new wing so the larger house was chosen.

Jessie did the hospital proud; Ambrose furnished it with some fine examples from leading London cabinet makers and the house acquired a personality. It was called Uvedale and it had it's own leather bound visitors book. Ambrose invited his brother to live with him and their widowed mother would eventually join them. Ambrose employed a personal maid, Elsie, but the house still felt empty. When it was finally finished, Ambrose and Jimmy did not want a grand opening; it was so good they did not want to publicise the fact they were the lucky ones to get to live there. Fortunately, their mother had not yet arrived. Whose idea had it been it to invite her?

The Committee had other ideas. Why not get the Duke of York to open Uvedale as well as the new wing? The house had attracted very favourable publicity in the architectural world; it was not every day that a smart London house was built from scratch, so there was tremendous interest in the detail inside as well as the exterior. The house did not disappoint – smart but not grand, it chimed with the times. Princess Louise came along as well and the Royal opening was incredibly popular as the great and the good flocked to see the detail. If the trade union sponsors had any misgivings, they did not show them, as the house began to exert its magic.

Alistair looked at the Visitors Book. The first signatures were the Duke of York and Princess Louise of Argyll.

They ended the visit with a cup of tea in Uvedale with the Committee, including Bertie and Joyce. Most were embarrassed by the Duke's stumbling speech, exacerbated by the public occasion. Bertie took him aside and as they talked, Bertie realised there was a lot more to the Duke than his stutter.

Eventually it was all over and Ambrose and Jimmy were left in the drawing room. Caterers had cleaned everything away so they were left alone. However, Ambrose had acquired a bottle of champagne, hidden in the recess of one of the cabinets he designed. There was also a cut glass decanter. "Mother will not find this," he said.

His brother looked round guiltily "Are you sure Ambrose?"

"Well, she's not here yet, come on, enjoy it." He poured them both a drink in new glasses.

"Here's to us, Uvedale is a masterpiece."

"Not bad, is it?" Said Jimmy, enjoying the drink.

Ambrose ducked out of the night out at the opera. Jimmy loved it and this time he got to meet the singer Muriel Richardson and he invited her out to dinner afterwards.

Bertie's official duties were not quite over. Ramsay Macdonald invited him to attend the Indian Round Table Conference in 1932. There were several press photos of the Conference and Bertie talking to various delegates.   Much to Bertie's surprise, Gandhi came across to see him. "Mr Lees-Smith, I believe."

"Yes sir."

"I have read your book on the Indian money supply."

"You must be the only one," said Bertie. "It's not exactly a bestseller." "You do yourself an injustice."

"You must come to tea." Said Bertie spontaneously "It's Indian and

I know it is picked in an unjust way."

"I think I will overlook it on this occasion." So Bertie telephoned Ambrose who was delighted to welcome them and the family at Uvedale. It was fascinating to hear Gandhi talk about South Africa and India. Then Bertie related how he had come to Britain at all; his father, an army major in the Indian Army, had died on the Northwest Frontier when Bertie was two. His mother had taken him and his two brothers, one older one younger, to see her father, his grandfather, a High Court judge in Bombay. He was about to retire and go back to live in England. He decided he could take only one of the brothers back to live with him and be educated. Despite being the middle one, Bertie was chosen, and so he had a 'full English' education.

He never forgot where he was born and he had gone back to Bombay for one year as a visiting professor. He had only managed to return to his birthplace once. He found it interesting but it was not the place of his imagination. "Some things are best left there", said Gandhi softly. "You're right."

"And your brothers?" Gandhi asked.

"I have hardly seen them at all but they both went to South Africa, as you did," said Bertie.

"We have more in common than you might think."

Bertie replied. "Why don't you come up to the North of England? I think you would be surprised how popular you would be."

"Always the lucky one." Joyce said afterwards.

"I didn't tell him about the Thuggees." Bertie replied.

"Thuggies?"

"They were an Indian sect who believed in assassinating people. My grandfather sentenced one of them to death. He was playing tennis and received a telegram but finished the game. The thuggee was hung and the next weekend grandfather was playing another game of tennis. He felt something in his pocket and read the telegram. The man had been reprieved. There was a row of course but grandfather kept his job."

"I'm glad you did not share that with Gandhi. I'm not so glad you shared it with me." Joyce poured herself another drink.

Another famous signature in the Visitor's Book.

The Woodhall boys had been too busy to meet her off the train, or said they were; typical, too busy to meet their frail old mother, Trefosa thought, we'll see about that. There was nothing for it but to get a taxi. Ambrose had said he would pay; yes, I'll make sure he does. The porter took her luggage to the taxi rank. "Uvedale please." she said crossly to the taxi driver; the man looked surprised. " Yes, Uvedale, Golders Green."

"Oh, I know where it is." He said as he got out and helped the porter with her bags. What a rude man, she thought.

Truth be told she had never actually been to London before. Manchester had been quite far enough. As they drove along, she was impressed by the buildings, yes, but also the bustle and the life. I'm going to like it here, she thought. The taxi took her to the door and the driver started taking her bags up the steps, she could not believe where she was; there were trees everywhere, behind the trees the hospital was so much larger and more impressive than the small cottage hospital in her mind. But it was the house that really captivated her – did her sons really live here? A servant was taking her cases inside, I could get used to this, she thought as Ambrose and Jimmy came down the steps to greet her – I am already. Uvedale had its first mistress.

There was the carefully wrapped cut glass decanter Ambrose had managed to conceal from his mother for all those years.

15 THE EVENING STANDARD

"What about Plodge?" Said Joyce, looking at the beautiful handwritten bill from Peterborough Lodge, Patrick and CJ's prep school. She inserted it carefully in Bertie's line of sight just in front of the Manchester Guardian. "Oh well, I'll just have to go back to the LSE like before. We'll get by," said Bertie.

"Oh no we won't, then there's Westminster next year, none of it's cheap, even with your ridiculous insistence they stay as day boys," said Joyce.

"I don't suppose they could spend all their time at Beech Court?" Bertie said weakly. Joyce glared at him.

Beech Court was Aunt Lily's own school for 50 girls in Walmer, Kent. Increasingly, parents were now making as much provision for their daughters as their sons. The girls came from all over the country and the Empire. Lily had never married but always remained close to Emma and had helped with the grandchildren in the family, especially after the sudden death of Sidney. Her nieces and nephews all led full lives, somewhat to the detriment of family life. All women over 21 had finally got the vote in 1928; as significant was the refusal of the new generation of middle class women just to stay at home and think of England occasionally, Emma's children were no different. The youngest, Christabel, had married a chartered accountant and had a daughter, Bridget. Percy and Dorothy had two girls and a boy. Joyce acted as Bertie's political secretary, as well as participating in all sorts of Labour party activities for women, both in London and Keighley. As the grandchildren got older, the school holidays got longer and more of a problem. All their parents had rejected the idea of boarding schools. Ironically it was during the school holidays the children got their chance to board as it became increasingly convenient to send them to Beech Court. They joined the girls whose parents were unable, or unwilling, to look after them during the holidays. Actually it was a great environment and they all loved it most of the time. Joyce's sister Marjory finally divorced Geoffrey and bought a house near Beech Court. Lily tried to help her to regain her self-confidence by encouraging her to help out at the school.

 Beech Court was not a solution to Bertie's financial problems. He did go back to the LSE but he thought of another trade as well. This is not 1918 when I was just the ex-second MP for Northampton; I've been a minister, that should count for something – and it did. As he did the rounds of newspaper editors he was treated with some respect and did get an invitation to write an article for the Evening Standard. "We'll see how this goes," said the editor.

"This is Jix's old stomping ground, we've crossed swords many a time, but he once did me a great favour – and he was a great character." Bertie was saying to Percy Holman.

Alistair looked up Jix: Sir William Joynson-Hicks, the Home Secretary, had put Bertie on the Parliamentary Committee for the Irene Savidge Inquiry and he had helped Irene herself back on her feet. The other Police 'victim' had been his old parliamentary neighbour, Leo Chiozza Money. A couple of years later off his own bat, Jix had put on a bravura Parliamentary performance to maintain that Cranmer's fine words in the Prayer Book were not to be tampered with and the official changes were overturned.

 Jix had been kicked upstairs to the Lords and Percy fought the subsequent Twickenham by-election for Labour. "Look, It's no good asking me to help you, Percy; I'm out, damaged goods, return to sender."

"Don't be ridiculous. I lost as well, remember."

"Twickenham is not exactly Labour territory; Keighley is – or was."

"It's no good just fighting where you think you can win easily; the party workers are very enthusiastic, they would love to meet you and Joyce." "I think she would like to mend a few fences with

Dorothy."

Bertie did enjoy helping Percy. They met Jix. "Lambeth Palace has stooped very low this time sending you, Bertie."

"They did promise fewer years less in Purgatory. More if we actually won. I hope the Bishops welcome you with Christian Charity."

"Not quite the Lost Sheep. But I have noticed a few crooks around." He replied.

It was not to be. In the end they lost by less than 5000 votes, not a bad result, he thought. I must be going soft, it was still second.

In the chest was a Church of England Prayer Book with Cranmer's original 1662 liturgy, signed by Jix. The Bishops never did warm to Jix.

He was just leaving the count when he was tapped on the shoulder. "May I talk to you?" Said a man in his 30s.

"Of course, why don't we have a pint round the corner."

When they were sitting down the man said. "I have come to thank you personally for what you did for Irene. She is my .... never mind."

Bertie began to say something but the man held up his hand. "No, you did right. I happen to be ... well ....in the security services, here is my card. Let's just call me the Fox. If there is ever anything I can do for you, please let me know."

And he got up in an unhurried way, turned round and just seemed to disappear into the crowd. When he thought about it afterwards, Bertie couldn't remember what the man even looked like; it was as if he had never existed, but he did keep the card.

Many other articles for of the Evening Standard followed. In 1934 Bertie managed to get a US tour.

Alistair was just spellbound as he read Bertie's article describing going round Al Capone's precinct in Chicago with the Police Captain.

There was another article criticising the idea of public schools and saying how many unhappy boarders he had met while he was Minister of Education. What a pity his own parents had not followed this advice, Alistair thought wistfully. There was an impressive pencil profile from Ginsbury, a fellow contributor to the Evening Standard.

There was one scoop Bertie did not pursue.

Although it would rarely travel more than a mile at a time a car had been specially ordered from Germany... and special it was, a brand new Mercedes staff car, complete with mechanics and full Nazi regalia.

The car swept out of the Embassy and made the short journey to Dean's Yard, the entrance to Westminster school. Ribbentrop, the new German ambassador, and his sons had expected to drive to the front door but a bicycle was leant against the wall of the gatehouse, effectively blocking their path. One of the guards got off the running board to move it, but it was securely locked to a bar in the wall. What was a small annoyance escalated to a major irritation as the school caretaker, when summoned, could do no more than the guard to move the offending bike. In the end they had to walk to the school entrance – it had just begun to rain to add to their discomfort. Ribbentrop was really annoyed but kept his temper. The bicycle had been chained to the wall in the precise place to cause maximum disruption by the longstanding maths teacher, Hope-Jones.

The Ribbentrops were shown round the school and Joachim's humour returned somewhat; this really was the heart of the establishment, he thought. Meanwhile rumours began to fly and in no time schoolboys were flocking round the car. The guards were a bit cautious at first, but they were not much older than the boys, whose natural enthusiasm soon overcame any suspicion. They were not allowed to touch but the chauffeur opened up the bonnet and they could see the engine and admire the purr as he started it up. When Joachim and his wife came back, they found the admiring crowd. Seizing the moment, Joachim said "Pretty good, boys, eh?" "Oh yes, Sir." The Ribbentrops drove off to a genuinely enthusiastic clap. Bertie listened as Patrick and Christopher told him the story. Patrick was genuinely knowledgeable about cars, writing letters to manufacturers and getting a lot of information in return but he had never rated a German car before.

Bertie was just getting his feet under the table at the Evening Standard when Stanley Baldwin called a General Election.

Bertie felt very alone in the overcrowded room where they were counting the votes. He had tried his best but he felt his meetings had lacked the spirit of previous years. There was a quiet confidence in the Conservative camp, they were far better funded and they looked – well, more modern and slick, including their candidate. I'd vote for him myself, he thought; he felt really old and tired. This is Sheffield all over again. Luckily the attention was focussed on the mounting piles of votes for each party and they were not looking good for Bertie. He felt the support draining away – whatever happens, I'm not putting myself through this again. He could almost feel himself getting ill. Claire did not look at all happy either. They seemed to have stopped counting the votes, the opposing camp were careful not to crow, but their pile definitely looked larger. Then Claire noticed a couple of boxes in the corner; the returning officer went over – they were definitely valid, uncounted votes, and Claire knew they had come from solid Labour wards. The Labour pile began to mount and it was the turn of the Conservative to look downcast. In the end Bertie won by 636 votes, the recount confirmed it, thank God. Bertie felt dog tired but had won by a whisker. Nationally Labour had come back from the dead and more than doubled its seats, but it was still only back where it had been 15 years ago and the government could steam on as if nothing had happened. But there was about to be a shock on a seismic constitutional scale.

16 THE CORONATION CHAIRS

Privy council meetings were an occasional welcome distraction and Bertie stayed in touch with Stanley Baldwin. Their paths came closer together in 1935 as Stanley became Prime Minister again and Bertie was narrowly returned to parliament. The Privy Council had the pleasant task of dispensing some joy round the Country for the Silver Jubilee of King George V. Perhaps sped along the way by his own doctor, the king died not long afterwards and the Privy Council began to meet in earnest and perform important constitutional tasks, including forming the Accession Council of Edward VIII.

In the meantime, Bertie had to attend the funeral of George V as a Royal Mourner. This was to be no trivial engagement. The planning was precise: the body would be transported by train to Kings Cross where there was a military guard of honour to meet it at 2.30 in the afternoon of 27th January 1936. An Officer and ten men of the King's Company Grenadier Guards would take the coffin off the train and mount it on a gun carriage. The Imperial Crown would be placed on top of the coffin. This carriage was to be drawn by the Royal Horse Artillery. There would be a procession to Westminster Hall where the coffin would be moved onto a Catafalque, where the king would lay in state. Two days later the coffin would be taken by train to the Kings final resting place in St Georges Chapel, Windsor.

The one thing that could not be planned for was the weather. It was cold, wet and windy as only it can be in London in January. Bertie waited in the rain, head bowed. Everyone had their hats off as a mark of respect. The train came in on time but the actions were all carried out with agonising, if appropriate, slowness. Eventually the procession started and continued, literally at the funeral rate of 12 paces a minute. Suddenly the cortege stopped. Bertie was already totally soaked and fed up. 'What is it now?' He peered forward through the rain. The Imperial Crown had fallen into the gutter. A soldier knelt to pick it up. He stood to attention to replace it on the coffin, saluted and then returned to his position. It was not a good omen. The courtege resumed it's slow pace. It took another age to reach Westminster Hall and over an hour to the first sheltered place. Many of the mourners were in fact old men and had really suffered from the cold and wet, not to mention the need for relief. It was never admitted but some never really recovered from the ordeal. Bertie had not felt so bad since his time at the Front twenty years before. He was absolutely soaked through. It was a while before he could get home and into a hot bath. After a good soak and a strong drink of whisky he felt a bit better, went to bed early and slept right through. Unfortunately the next day he had to go back to file past the coffin again. There were some notable absences. The weather was not quite so bad as the previous day but again he got cold and wet. Once more he returned home for a hot bath and whisky. The third day began well as it was not actually raining. This time he had to go to Windsor Station and wait bareheaded before the coffin arrived. Unknown to him there had been a slight accident and the Royal Train had been held up. They stood for three hours. It began to drizzle after one hour and the weather gradually got worse. The sky went very black and there was a tremendous thunderstorm. Nobody moved. Eventually the coffin arrived and the mourners escorted it to St Georges Chapel. It took much longer to get back home from Windsor. By the time Bertie returned, he was seriously ill, way beyond a hot bath. He went straight to bed with a high temperature. He was still ill the next morning so Joyce called for help. A young doctor arrived and panicked, which did not help Bertie. But the doctor arranged an immediate consultation in Harley Street with a visiting Doctor from America, who prescribed a new powerful but untested course of tablets called Ebrymol. "The very latest." He was all reassurance.

There was a regular meeting of the Manor House Board. Ambrose was describing his new groundbreaking work in keyhole surgery. Bertie was still in bed so Joyce attended in his place. Afterwards Ambrose asked after Bertie and listened to what had happened with mounting concern. When he heard about Ebrymol, he had difficulty hiding his horror under a professional mask. This was scandalous mistreatment for monetary gain. "Let me see him immediately." Joyce looked worried. "No fees, just as a friend," said Ambrose quickly. "But please on no account give him any more pills."

Joyce was impressed with his professionalism and his concern. They looked at each other and there was a brief spark of recognition. At least he was a Baronet, Joyce thought to herself; Oh how naughty you are!

Bertie survived the illness but his heart was never quite the same again. He was now invited onto the committee to arrange Edward VIII's coronation. This was a highly contentious poisoned chalice: to accommodate the undivorced Wallis Simpson, the Coronation was planned to take place in the neutral atmosphere of the Banqueting House of Whitehall rather than the traditional religious location of Westminster Abbey.

In the midst of all this Bertie managed to beat Charles Trevelyan in the Rearmament debate at the Labour Party Conference. Otherwise Labour MPs would have been mandated to vote against any sort of rearmament, come what may. He and Bertie remained friends but the Top Hats were falling apart.

But there was mounting unease in the ruling elite about the behaviour of King Edward who seemed to deliberately defy all convention. Wallace Simpson was a problem that could not be brushed over easily and now was blazoned all over the Foreign Press. Although Baldwin managed to keep the Press Barons to a self-imposed silence, this could not last forever. The rebel in Bertie thought the King should be left alone but the churchman saw that this was not possible, so he largely supported the Baldwin line. He knew, but did not get involved with, the lengths that the Establishment went to prevent Mrs Wallis Simpson from becoming Queen, Consort, or whatever to the King. Joyce was much more sympathetic to Edward.

In the chest Alistair found a copy of the Osbert Sitwell poem Rat's Week which described how all the friends of Edward and Wallis had deserted them in their hour of need. Although only typed, Joyce had written that it was one of only twenty copies. Rare ....and perhaps dangerous to keep at the time.

Baldwin knew that Bertie could have been a formidable antagonist. Partially due to Edward's visit to Dowlais, once the largest ironworks in Europe and now totally abandoned, he was largely popular with the workers and therefore Bertie's relative silence was helpful. Eventually Edward was cornered into abdicating and the problem was solved for Baldwin, albeit at the expense of not paying sufficient attention to a growing host of international problems.

Baldwin offered Bertie the ultimate accolade in his gift. One evening they were having a drink at the Athenaeum after yet another Privy Council meeting. "Bertie, I'd like to make you a peer."

Bertie thought it was a joke but when he looked him in the eye, he saw he was serious. He did not say anything. "Think about it," said Baldwin soothingly.

"Don't worry, I will. There will be .... implications. I'll let you know tomorrow."

"Please do, I hope you accept," said Baldwin with genuine warmth.

Bertie could hardly believe it. He did all the London things he so loved. He walked to the tube. It was a cold evening but he was wrapped up well and hardly aware of it. Everybody was just getting on with their business. A queue was beginning to form at a new show at the theatre. Some foolhardy newsboys were still shouting their wares. He loved the great buildings, had done since he had first come to England. He was being offered an honourable retirement from the hurly-burly of the House of Commons where your career could end just like that. Joyce would absolutely love it.

He knew her well enough, who wouldn't - his constituents. They would feel betrayed, think that he had taken advantage of them to cash in his chips. They could … they would get someone else. He'd been an MP on and off for over 25 years. Truth was he was feeling his age a lot more these days. He sometimes felt ill for no reason. He hadn't told the electorate of course. He had just managed to claw back the seat. He knew he could not fight another election. He reached the tube and went down the escalator. Someone was trying their luck with a violin. He wasn't bad at all. He gave him some silver coins. He could hear the reassuring echo of a train. It slid to a halt. The doors opened, people got out and there was that urgent ticking as the train waited impatiently for all the passengers to embark. Then it whooshed off into the blackness. Four stations. Bertie laughed out loud. There was no one close enough to hear him. He had no money. If MPs were poorly paid, then their Lordships got literally nothing. He knew a number of his colleagues who had been 'kicked upstairs' and regretted it. Some lived on charity. There were only so many free dinners you could go to before the novelty wore off. The trouble was that no one believed that politicians could be poor. But in the absence of lining your own pocket that is indeed what you became. There was always the Evening Standard but that seemed too fickle. Joyce once had a little money but that was long gone though she was still trying to sue members of her family for imagined sums she thought rightfully hers. He would still have to lecture. That would cause mirth or derision amongst students. Probably both. But what would he do in old age if he ever reached it? When he felt ill he thought he'd got there already. Up to now he had hardly considered it. All his thoughts had been with Joyce, twenty years younger. What had he to offer now he was getting older? Well: a peerage might help.

He got off at his stop and walked up the hill. He had made up his mind not to tell Joyce about the offer at all because he knew it would end in disappointment, whatever happened. But as they had a drink together later, he just could not resist. She was really surprised and congratulated him very warmly. He thought she had looked a bit depressed recently, as if she thought that he would need an increasing amount of nursing care. Those damn pills, he had never felt right since taking them. After a while she said: "You weren't going to tell me, were you. You thought I'd get upset if you didn't accept the Peerage... yes, I would be upset. Of course I'd like the position. The Buxtons took it. Margaret even took over Noel's seat."

"Keighley is not Norwich. She's lost it since. Would you want to do it?"

"I don't know. I do know we can't afford just to accept the peerage. I'm actually upset because I know you deserve it and not just because of your friendship with Stanley. Because of everything you've done over the years. It's just a pity it does not come with any kind of pension. Anyway you are missing a vital point."

"What's that?"

"You are not thinking, Bertie. For once I'm way ahead of you."

"Not for the first time! What do you mean?"

"Patrick."

"Patrick?"

"Yes, if you are made a peer, he'll inherit in time. I think we should ask him. It'll affect him more than you."

Somewhat chilling, Bertie thought. "We'll ask him tomorrow"

"Why not now; he's not a little boy; It's Friday, he's just doing Latin homework, I'm sure he won't mind a break."

They called him down and Bertie gently told him of the offer. "Look, I know I'm always trying to give you advice but this really is your choice."

"So, I would become an Honorable immediately."

"Yes, I suppose you would."

"There are some Honorables at school. They are teased horribly."

"Now you are beginning to see some of the problems."

"You'll get a lot more money though," said Patrick helpfully.

"No, none actually. I'll still have to lecture and I'll get teased like you, only more so! ...But being a Lord is still something. It will be of immense value to you if you can carry it off.... and to your eldest son."

"Dad, really,' said Patrick reddening.

"Look, Patrick you know the position. Your mother and I are leaving it to you. You've a lot to think about. Tell us in the morning. What would Caesar have done?"

"Someone would have stabbed him in the back before he could have a chance to do anything!"

Patrick was not happy at school. His parents, or rather his father, had insisted that he and his younger brother be day boys. He thought he stuck out like a sore thumb. He and Christopher would have been fine boarding. More independent of Mum and Dad but he guessed more vulnerable to the sometimes incessant bullying that went on. Of course they teased him over his Labour father. And they would tease him even more about being an Honorable, Labour and a Day Boy, a dubious triple reason for being singled out. He did not want to stick out even more.

But that wasn't the main problem. Patrick's writing in his journal was hesitant at first but soon became more confident and assured. He had been an ardent supporter of the League of Nations; he had joined the local branch and had written essays for them that had won prizes. Here was the thing. The League of

Nations just did not work. Japan and Italy blatantly ignored their resolutions. And there did not seem anything anybody could do about it peacefully or otherwise. Now, right at this minute, the Fascist Coup against the democratically elected, if left-wing, Spanish Republican Government was being halted. The Italian and German International Brigades were battling it out with the Italian Army and the Condor Legion, house by house, room by room in the University City of Madrid. Ne Pasaran... They shall not pass. Patrick loved the slogans; 'It's Better to Die on your Feet than Live on your Knees.'

And now he was suddenly confronted with the prospect of becoming a Lord. Instinctively he knew he couldn't 'carry it off' as his father had put it. Christopher could, no problem. But it wasn't something you could just hand on if it didn't suit. Even if it were possible, CJ would be even more insufferable.

And Spain: he was seventeen. He could go. He loved his parents but it wasn't that that was stopping him. He had been in the first eleven at football but then a sudden attack of measles had nearly killed him and left him very nearly blind as well as much less fit. So he knew he would be of little use to the Spanish Republic.

No, he could not be a peer. It would break his mother's heart but he hoped she would see the wisdom of it. She never quite did.

"Still the rebel, eh Bertie." Baldwin said. "More complicated than that I'm afraid"

"Money eh? I'm sure we can set you up with a nice little sinecure. How are you with Stools?"

"I did enough of that at the Front!" I'll even pay you myself. No strings attached." Bertie knew Baldwin was in fact very generous and had never accepted any public salary, But he could imagine the headlines. "I do appreciate the offer but my son just does not want it."

"Patrick, fine boy, Christopher would though."

"You're right there. Why did you offer me the peerage, was it the Abdication or the War estimates?"

Baldwin looked at him for a while, "Neither, actually, I've always admired what you've done."

Bertie was visibly taken aback.

"And I don't want any favours in the future either," continued Baldwin, "Am I not too old to be joining the Conservative party?" Asked Bertie.

"I don't think so," replied Baldwin."Anyway I'm leaving myself – I haven't told anybody else, only one other person, actually."

"Please can you just sit there, I'm still on the books of the Evening Standard, this scoop will set me up for life."

"I would rather you didn't, it's deniable. I'm probably not leaving the Conservative party but I am leaving the House of Commons."

"Really, I hate to admit it but if there was a General Election tomorrow you'd wipe the floor with us."

"Thanks to passing the Estimates bill, we are now re-arming on a massive scale. I used to believe that the bomber would always get through but now the RAF has a real chance of stopping them with these brand new fighters and detection equipment, but it all requires a lot of money. It will take time to build up a critical mass of squadrons to defend London."

"That was well hidden in the Bill."

"Oh, it's all top secret but frankly I've had enough, I'm a peaceful man, I just like warm beer in a nice English country pub on a Sunday watching cricket. – I'm not interested in foreign affairs. So I'm going upstairs and leaving it to ...." he paused "Oh, you'll know soon enough – Neville."

"Neville Chamberlain?"

"Not too many Nevilles on the front bench last time I looked – yes him"

"Oh he just didn't come to mind."

"Don't underestimate him."

"You didn't think Churchill?"

"Can't stand the man; that doesn't rule him out though. The Cabinet would be very small if it just included my friends."

"I'd join."

"Thanks, but you are a bit ahead of your time, Bertie, for either of our parties. No, I did think about it but he behaved so badly during the General Strike, I thought we'd lose it."

"The TUC lost it by themselves – and he won't be remembered so well in Llanelli either."

"Indeed not, people have long memories. Consensus politics will do for now. Hopefully we do still have a couple of years of peace left. If you do change your mind about the peerage, I'm still here for a little while. I think you owe me a nice glass of port."

Bertie and Joyce attended the 1937 Coronation in Westminster Abbey. and in the chest was the imposing invitation from the Earl Marshal. Joyce loved the ceremony but she reflected they would have got a much better view if Bertie had been a Lord; Lady Lees-Smith of North End, it would have worked. *They had been given the two upholstered chairs they sat on during the ceremony. They were now in Alistair's hall.*

17 BEECH COURT

"This is for you," said Joyce, disapprovingly, as she handed him a letter from Germany. Adolph Hitler stared at him uncompromisingly from the stamp. I'm too old to be called up now, Bertie thought, and certainly not by you. He opened the expensive vellum envelope with his silver paper knife and extracted the letter. It had a beautiful coat of arms and an address in old German script, the only bit of which he could decipher was Frankfurt.

Luckily the rest of the letter was in English, handwriting vaguely remembered. It was several pages long but before reading it he turned to the end. It was from Gunter Schmidt, his ex-student and the young officer he had rescued.

Gunter was now married with two children and was a senior banker in the Reichbank. He was coming to London on business and would Bertie like to meet him?

Of course he would. So a couple of weeks later they were sitting with a drink on the terrace of the House of Commons, overlooking the Thames. "The Mother of Parliaments." Gunter said.

"Just about," said Bertie.

"How is Percy?" Asked Gunter.

"He's fine, he's running his father's paper business – not as good quality as your letter," said Bertie. "I married his sister".

"Marjorie? Christobel?"

"Neither. Joyce, we have two sons, 18 and 16."

"Sons, what to do with them eh?" Said Gunter. "Actually, I do have a request. Bertie, I have always respected what you stood for at the LSE." "Glad you remembered," replied Bertie.

"And that was before you rescued me!" They clinked wine glasses.

"I'm sorry, you just won't get used to our beer," said Bertie. Gunter was enjoying the wine and looking at the reflections in the river. After a while he said. "I do have a favour to ask; my son, Lothar is also 18, every spare moment he is with the Hitler Youth. I am not political, nor is the Bank, but Greta and I are concerned about him. Anna is 16 but more independent."

"I see," said Bertie, "How can I help?"

"I thought a spell in England would give him a different perspective ..... before it is too late."

"Too late?"

"I'm sorry, Bertie, you are ever the optimist. Life is fine here but if you came to Germany you would see a big difference."

"You want Lothar to stay with us?" Bertie asked.

"Just for a month, maybe two, in the summer." Bertie thought for a bit. "Look, Patrick and CJ go and stay in Beech Court every summer." He described it to Gunter. "Well It is certainly better than the youth camp he would be going to otherwise."

"I bet they sing good songs, though," said Bertie." Just let me know where to meet Lothar."

But Gunter had not finished. "And in return."

"There's no need for that," said Bertie.

"Patrick can come over to Frankfurt the next year – I will give him a job in the Reichsbank and they will find a flat for him."

"Good Lord, that is a fantastic offer. I know things may seem peaceful but I too am worried about what Patrick might do in the future; this is a huge opportunity, I must discuss this with Joyce. If

I can arrange it you can come to dinner at Uvedale. This is part of a hospital that was started during the last war, a very small legacy of good."

And there was a German signature in the visitors' book.

Alistair opened a cardboard box labelled Beech Court in the corner of the chest. In it there were some photos and exercise books, mostly filled with forgotten passages from Caesar's Gallic Wars, isosceles triangles and doodles such as imagined signatures of Claudette Colberg and other distant stars. One of the exercise books told the story of Lothar's visit in neat, clear handwriting. Although the author was clearly young and female with a flair for writing. Was it the young Bridget? Alistair never found out.

The visit was not an unqualified success. To be honest, Lothar just did not fit in. It was his personality rather than the fact that he was German. He missed home a lot and his comrades in the Hitler Youth even more. He was stiff and formal in the German way.

To be fair 'joining in' meant the Boy Scouts. Lothar said. "This is banned in Germany, I cannot join."

To CJ, who had the Gilwall woggle, this was betrayal. However, there was no escape from the Walmer War Club, this was open to girls as well as boys and all nationalities were welcome, so Lothar was a reluctant recruit, and joined in British triumphs from ages past. The French were the usual villains, but Henry V and the trapped English army usually managed to fight their way out against overwhelming odds at Agincourt. There were occasional swipes at the Scots and the Spanish but the French were the main foe as Britain and Marlborough tried to keep the balance of power against Louis XIV at Blenheim. Later Wellington defended the small nations in the Peninsular War against Napoleon and then Lothar was very welcome as Blucher yet again managed to relieve the Duke at the 11th hour, World War 1 was politely forgotten.

However, he was different and quite good looking and the girls did find him a challenge. One of them managed to smuggle a bottle of wine into the school and inveigled Lothar into a laundry cupboard in a part of the school closed for the holidays. They got drunk and both lost their virginity; the girl liked the experience but Lothar was disgusted with himself and it did not enhance his love of Britain. He went back to Germany as committed to the Hitler Youth as ever.

There was another scrawled exercise book. Alistair recognised as an early version of CJ's writing.

It started with proceedings from the Walmer war club and tea and buns at aunt Marjory's; all sounded perfect, but Marjory was a troubled soul and began to confide in CJ. He was gaining in maturity and recognised something very deep in her. Not long after Lothar's return to Germany CJ was there when Geoffrey visited. There was a violent scene which CJ tried to break up but they both turned on him and he returned to Beech Court.

The summer sojourn at Beech Court had been cut short suddenly and it was some time before CJ knew what had happened.

The day after his visit, Marjory had been found lying in the flower bed, having fallen from her bedroom on the first floor. There was no investigation; Geoffrey's visit was not mentioned, perhaps not even known about; the verdict was that she took her own life while the balance of her mind was disturbed. CJ felt the full weight of responsibility; he might have stopped the fight or said something about Geoffrey's visit. He had done neither.

18 FRANKFURT

Stanley Baldwin still had inside information which he shared with Bertie. He was aware that when Neville Chamberlain flew off to Bad Godesburg on the first summit with Hitler, the essential critical mass of fighter squadrons to defend London did not yet exist… and no Prime Minister would take that risk. The resulting agreement with Hitler over Czechoslovakia was not surprising but Bertie knew that Britain would fight sooner or later. With a heavy heart, he and Joyce summoned Patrick and CJ, then 18 and 17. Alistair imagined the sober conversation. The boys would have to grow up quickly. One of the by-products of this was the strong advice to keep personal journals. The family made an agreement that these would be confidential and kept for posterity in a safe place.

A few weeks before, Joyce suffered food poisoning from eating a pie in a Lyons Corner House. When she recovered she was very angry because Bertie had done nothing about it.

She went round to Ambrose at Uvedale and said: "You deal with this sort of thing every day." He went with her to Lyon's head Office and they came away with a two week cruise at the company's expense in return for her silence. Feeling as if she had earned it, she went round to Liberty's to indulge herself with something naughty. She fell in love with the Chinese chest. It could even house all the journals. Unfortuneately it couldn't be delivered immediately. Never mind. Maybe Chamberlain was right and they did have time. She kept the 1938 Liberty's receipt.

Patrick had just left school. What was he to do? Republican Spain was all but finished. The International Brigades had been disbanded and the survivors were on their way home. Patrick was beginning to join in his mother's soirees held both in North Square and Uvedale. Their friends often dropped round and most took great interest in him and Christopher when they were around. He was fully aware what his father had done in the First World War.

He was in no doubt that he would be called up. The question was how he would respond. One of his father's friends, Lord Arnold, a Quaker and sincere pacifist, became his mentor and offered him a lifeline in the form of adopting him as his son in return for not fighting. As he was a millionaire with no children this was no mean offer; his father had made no comment. But would that be the cowards way? Despite everything, Patrick was still in the League of Nations Association. He had no sympathy with Mosley and the Fascists, although many of his friends did. Ribbentrop's son at school was not a good advert, neither was Lothar, although Patrick had got on with him well enough at Beech Court. These questions went round and round in his head. And he had to live, even make a living. It was too soon to go to University, not that he felt like it. It seemed like a way of deferring decisions. Out of the blue a job offer arrived from the Reichsbank in Frankfurt. Patrick soon realised that it was not totally unexpected but had come from Gunter, whom his father had saved and befriended. They had kept in touch and met occasionally when Gunter came to London on business. Patrick liked him. The idea of going to Frankfurt took hold very rapidly and solved the immediate quandary of what to do while waiting to see what happened on the International Front. He might not like Hitler and the Nazi Party but going to Germany would be very fascinating and challenging; a real experience.

So very soon he was packed up and on the boat train. He would never forget the journey to Frankfurt as he swished through Europe with everything to look forward to.

He immediately fell in love with the old city. The bank had found him a flat not too far from the centre and the office. Most of his colleagues were friendly, if a little formal. Patrick spoke some German and most of his colleagues a little English, some very well. A few chose not to speak at all. He found German workers and bosses cooperated much better than in Britain. Gunter invited him round to Sunday dinner. Patrick brought a small gift which was gratefully accepted by Gunter's wife, Greta, who was really welcoming. Lothar was very polite and friendly in his own way but was still in the Hitler Youth, clearly a Nazi well on the way to being fanatical. His sister Anna was also in the Hitler Youth but much more friendly ... and attractive. And there was Dinka, a maid who lived in an outhouse. She never got used to Patrick or liked him. On the other hand there was a good local Riesling which Patrick found he liked very much. Patrick and Anna got on well and Patrick was invited again the following week.

When Patrick presented another gift, Greta said there was no need as he was now a friend. Lothar was at a Hitler Youth weekend, which, to be honest, improved the atmosphere. As did a few glasses of Riesling. It was a lovely afternoon. Gunter's brother Reinhard dropped in and joined them. He was in the Gestapo but clearly unsympathetic to the Nazi Party, unlike his children. They shook Patrick's hand politely but then they had to leave early for yet another tribute to Horst Wessel.

Everybody went out into the garden which was not far from the river Main. There was a tiny viewing platform with just enough room for one. Greta invited Patrick to climb up to the top. It seemed to Patrick just the right distance because you could see across the river and right into the medieval wooden inner city. Small figures were going about their business and Patrick imagined traders selling their wares centuries ago when merchants would ply their trade up and down the water. Now and then, large barges passed effortlessly by. He loved the sun on the surface picking out the ripples of the current.

"Are you asleep up there? If you want some more wine, you had better come down."

"Coming," he said and climbed down. "Such a terrific view."

"Do you want to walk to the river?" Anna asked innocently.

"That would be lovely," he said as he looked into her blue eyes for the first time. She held his glance for a moment before lowering her gaze and reddening slightly. They got up to go. Gunter began to rise but Greta motioned him to stay seated. Anna led him to the back gate and they walked down the quiet street. He took hold of Anna's hand. They crossed over, went along a few yards and then down another road at the end of which was the river. Patrick stopped when they reached it but Anna said. "This way." They walked down a towpath to the right. There was a bench with a good view. Half a mile further up to the right there was a large bridge with little traffic but trams regularly clanked across in both directions. They sat down. Patrick was enjoying the scene when he felt Anna pull him towards her and they kissed. It was his first proper kiss, and maybe hers too. Patrick had his eyes closed but opened them after a while. She looked so beautiful. He felt very warm.

"I love you," he said.

"I know. I love you too," They held each other as the water flowed past. The moment seemed to last forever.

At last Anna said. "'Let's go on." They walked slowly towards the bridge and then stopped at a cafe and Patrick ordered two hot chocolates. They talked a lot about their dreams and hopes very naturally as if they had known each other a long time. They seemed to have a lot in common and politics and difficult subjects just disappeared. The chocolate was piping hot but delicious.

"I think we have to go back now. My parents will think you have kidnapped me." "I suppose I have," he said and she laughed.

Over the next couple of weeks their friendship blossomed. Greta was happy for them. Gunter was neutral but did not demur although you would have been very naive not to see the problems facing the couple. 'Did I say couple. They are not a couple yet', he thought grimly. Lothar was almost downright hostile. Patrick could see he thought that Anna should 'keep herself' for a 'pure' Aryan. However in the family he was overruled and the pair were allowed to grow together. Outside it was different. Even in somewhat introverted Frankfurt the Nazis were increasingly prominent and vocal. There were rallies and songs. The atmosphere steadily worsened although Patrick did find some of the songs very good to listen to and moving if you ignored the words and the aggressive marching. But that was impossible of course. Jews were beginning to be attacked openly in the streets and many were moving to the ghetto in Hanau. Patrick could only imagine what other discrimination there was. He was walking down a street and had just passed a postbox. He noticed an old man with a yellow armband rushing towards him. The Jew was so excited he failed to acknowledge the Hitler Youth on the other side of the road. Unfortunately the Youth noticed his lapse and strolled across.

"Where are you going in such a hurry, you rat?" (polite translation)

"Nowhere, your Honour." The Jew said unconvincingly.

"Don't lie to me," The Youth reached into the old man's pocket and extracted a letter. He looked at the British address. The Jew was really shaking.

The Youth turned towards Patrick and then back to the Jew. "Do you know what day it is?" He asked. The Jew shook his head.

"It's my birthday." The Jew was beginning to mumble congratulations but the Youth continued. "I'll let you post your letter but don't think your salvation will come from London."

Patrick's relationship with Anna blossomed. They went to some great concerts and Anna took him round all the Art Galleries. And then round again…

One day they took the train to Heidelburg and walked around the old town and Patrick had a full stein served by buxom barmaid who smiled at him. "'Don't get any ideas." Anna warned. Patrick laughed. They walked over the bridge and looked at the ruined Schloss on the hill. Patrick thought he could not be happier. They returned through the University quarter and he could not believe his ears; there actually were some students singing a traditional song together.

They went up the Rhine. Patrick got deliriously drunk as is only possible in Rudesheim. They took a cruise on a little paddle streamer. It was a lovely evening and they could see the lights of the little towns reflections twinkling in the river as the sun sank behind the cliffs. Patrick had some difficulty keeping his balance even though the current was gentle. They both just laughed and laughed.

In September there was the Wine festival. Not even the Nazis could stand in the way of Frankfurters relishing their autumn yield of grapes which did seem particularly good that year. Anna and he were enjoying a lovely evening in a street market. There was a German band in full traditional dress playing folksongs, the crowd singing along. Patrick was trying to join in when Anna pulled his arm.

"Come this way." They boarded a tram to the Stadtwald where they alighted and walked through the woods. "This is beautiful." Said Patrick. They turned down a side path into a small clearing, where she put her arms round him and kissed him. "It is time." And just in case he was in any doubt, she took off her blouse. He moved towards her and held her against him.

They made love among the pines. Patrick discovered her body gently at first, then very vigorously finished the act. It was very beautiful and they both fell asleep in an exhausted embrace. It was dark when they woke up; they looked up at the stars and made love again. Eventually they got up and raced to catch the last tram. They were not aware of anything else around them. He walked her home. They kissed again before he reluctantly departed. The streets were quiet but he could not describe how happy he felt, nothing else seemed to matter at all. Just Anna and him. He felt his whole life had been a prologue for this one evening. He opened the door to his flat. On the doormat was a letter from his father.

19 THE FOX

This was Alistair's favourite photograph: October 24 1938, Queen Mary is getting out of the royal car outside Uvedale. Ambrose is going down the steps to meet her. She is visiting Manor House Hospital to open another brand new wing of 50 beds. Bertie and Joyce are standing at the top of the steps. The press photo captured perfectly the cheering crowd and the joy of the moment.

Taking tea in Uvedale afterwards, Queen Mary questioned why Ambrose hadn't married. Luckily his mother Trefosa was not in the room but Bertie noticed Joyce blushing deeply.

Later he was alone in the house in North Square. He went into the study. Joyce's journal lay open. He wanted to read it but they had all agreed their journals would be confidential. What was the point anyway? Joyce was still young and must take every chance of happiness. He was not well. Perhaps refusing the peerage had been a mistake. The relationship with Joyce had been strained since her return from the cruise to Madeira, with a long cigarette holder and a taste for Sobranie; they were both worried about what would happen to Patrick and CJ. Soon all Bertie would be able to offer her would be nursing experience.

Then there was a knock on the door.

Bertie invited in a handsome man who looked much younger than his admitted age of 60. He was undoubtedly a Russian. He did seem familiar although Bertie could not place him. Count Nickolai Sambor introduced himself. They sat down in the drawing room where they had a view out the French windows. It was a nice evening and the garden enjoyed the last of the sun. A butterfly moved gracefully from flower to flower. After a short while Nickolai spoke. "It is very beautiful here."

"Yes," said Bertie. "'Hard to imagine there are any problems. But please explain why you have come. No, please tell me your own story first."

"I am Russian. Well, I was Russian a long time ago. I am a Russian Count. Once a Count, always a Count, eh. But on the wrong side for you, I think."

"I don't discriminate," said Bertie. "Please go on."

"My father was a great admirer of the English way of life so before the First World War I sent my daughter to be educated at Oxford. Life was so different then, so international. My daughter used to travel all over Europe on the Orient Express to Grand Balls. She fell in love with a young German Baron, also a Jew. They live in Frankfurt."

"But what happened to you?"

"I was in the Czars army and then I fought for the Whites in the plains of Southern Russia. I was captured and put up against a wall to be shot. Just then a biplane flew over. The peasants had never seen one and fled in terror - I took the opportunity to escape. I got first to Odessa and eventually got to England. I lived with my daughter and then managed to make another good living here. I am now proudly British."

Bertie was imagining the vast Russian landscape. "Thank you. I'm really interested to meet you. How can I help you? You know I am just a humble MP as caught up in events as you are."

"Well, I believe you are not without influence as we say. I know you are sympathetic to our cause."

"What cause is that, may I ask?" Said Bertie hesitantly.

"The treatment of the Jews in Germany."

"Yes, as you know I and others have asked the government to help but neither they nor any other major European power have chosen to intervene, at least not publically – or even privately as far as I know."

"No, I realise but we need your help."

"How, specifically?"

"One hundred British passports."

"What?" Bertie was genuinely taken aback. He had been spellbound by the story and his imagination had still been roaming the Steppes but this was a total shock and brought him crashing into the present.

"Please repeat what you just said."

"We need one hundred British passports."

"Right, you expect me to go the Foreign Secretary ... yes I do know him... and he will give me one hundred passports?"

"Well not exactly," said the Count.

"I thought not." Bertie was wide awake now. "You will have to tell me the whole story or this conversation ends, you can find someone else."

"We can't."

"That desperate, eh. I'm your last choice."

"No, you are the only choice."

"And why would that be?"

"Look... I do trust you, that's why I'm here. But this is unofficial, private." said Nickolai struggling for the right word.

"Go on."

"We have someone in the Foreign Office on the inside who can get us the passports."

"I'm sure it's not Halifax."

"No."

"What can you do with a blank passport anyway."

"They can just be completed with a signature and a photo and a family can get out. But we have to get the passports to Germany."

"Why don't you just post them. Look, I'll supply the stamps. Should be there in no time."

"No they check the parcel post now, especially packages."

"Oh no, I'm not going to Germany now. I like to remember it as it was. Anyway they'll search me for sure." "He paused..."No, not the diplomatic bag. You overestimate my power. What happens when the passports get there? They'd search anybody going near the embassy let alone coming out with a package."

"They would not search your son."

"Whoa, wait a minute."

Another genuine shock that a stranger knew his son was in Germany. He looked at the man and got an inkling of the desperation that had led him into their drawing room. He could not be angry.

The passports were to be delivered by diplomatic bag to the Consulate in Frankfurt where by coincidence Patrick was now working. He indeed could go to the Consulate without hindrance. Bertie asked for an assurance that this action was not for financial gain: "For myself, no. I just want to help my family and others. In Frankfurt I cannot say. These are dangerous times."

Just then Joyce returned and joined them. They had a drink, in fact several over the night. The Count introduced himself and Joyce listened intently.

She asked: "Was your daughter called Olga?"

"Yes."

"Well I'm sure I saw you both at one of the Balls in London, one of the few I went to before the war...or after for that matter." Bertie looked guilty.

"Of course, the Trevelyan's Ball. It was beautiful. But surely you are too young to have been there?"

"Thank you, I was only a girl, I remember Olga, She looked radiant. You didn't look so bad, either!" The Count blushed a little.

"And she is in Germany now?"

"Yes."

Joyce looked at the two men. "Bertie's right. We must try to help." She paused ...'I did not know you had access to the diplomatic bag. I could have done with some more 4711."

"I don't, darling."

"Never trust a politician," she said. Both men looked at each other, realised the drink had got to her and they all laughed heartily.

Bertie said. "I may be able to help you but you must not ask questions. I have to trust you too." Nickolai nodded. "If I can help to get the passports to Frankfurt, my son will need to pass them on to a reliable person in a secure place."

"It will be arranged." They shook hands as friends.

It was time to meet the Fox. The next morning he took a taxi to Whitehall and left a message to meet 'Uncle Frank' at the Spaniards on Hampstead Heath later that day.

"Another Hospital meeting, Sir?" Asked Peter, the Landlord.

"It's Bertie and you know it. Look, I'm meeting someone. Can I sit outside and not be disturbed. Please come out and offer us another drink if you think there is anybody out of the ordinary."

Peter nodded and put his finger to his nose.

"Well, if it's not Uncle Bertie." Came a jocular voice. "Let's have some Youngers together and talk about old times." They went to a table outside and had a hearty cheese sandwich to accompany the ale.

After some small talk, the Fox relaxed with his drink. "I don't mind telling you Bertie, I've gone a few steps up the ladder so I do some interesting things now. What can I help you with?"

When Bertie explained about putting a package in the Diplomatic Bag to Frankfurt, the Fox looked worried. "'Heydrich and the SD." He said. "They are very good. The main Embassy is alright because we've laid things on the line to Ribbentrop. Tit for tat. If they open ours we'll open theirs. And we can tell. But consulates are wide open and the SD is closing in on the Jews so I don't rule out their looking at our bags. To be honest, we have no way of knowing."

He could see the mention of Jews drew a frown from Bertie. This was growing murkier by the day but he had given his word.

"I can see I'll have to go myself."

"Hang on, Bertie, hang on there, I can see you are serious. I do not know your reasons but you helped us out once and I want to return the favour. I will take it myself, I'm owed some leave. I speak German, I can get the package to Berlin via the diplomatic bag, no problem. I can fly to Berlin and then deliver it to your son in Frankfurt. It's just a package to me. I don't know what's in it and I do not want to know. Get a Rare Books label to put on it." Bertie was amazed how cannily close 'Uncle Frank' was to guessing the nature of the package.

"I cannot let you go." Bertie said. "It's not your problem."

"Your problem is mine. Whatever your son needs he will get. Don't forget the Fox has not got caught yet."

Bertie told Nickolai that he could deliver the passports to Patrick in Frankfurt. They both realised that it would be safer if Bertie himself picked up the passports from their man inside the Foreign Office. A meeting was arranged in a busy cafe near Westminster. Bertie was surprised to find that their man was in fact an attractive young woman. She put the package down by the table and they had a cup of tea together. "I'm sorry the rules have changed. Our limit has been cut down to fifty … I only got forty so as not to attract suspicion."

"Can I pay you for them?"

"No, I do not want anything, thanks."

"Well, I cannot imagine what you've been through but I can tell you these will save lives." She got up and walked out and disappeared into the crowd.

After a while, Bertie himself rose and picked up the package. He felt very vulnerable as he was putting himself and his reputation on the line. The cafe was still busy so nobody noticed him go. He walked down the street trying not to look round to see if he was being followed. The package was inconspicuous and looked exactly right for rare books. After three hundred yards, he stopped at a shop window and looked in the reflection for a couple of minutes. No one was to be seen. Feeling safer he caught the tube back to Highgate.

Bertie invited Nickolai to his house and showed him the package. He was naturally very disappointed. They had a drink and then another. Nickolai did begin to relax.

"Well it's much more portable. I'm not sure I could have managed one hundred passports. I was afraid in case I was being followed."

"Of course. Thank you for getting them. You have put yourself at risk."

"It's just the beginning. The package still has a long way to go." They both looked at it.

"It's hard to believe how important such a little parcel could be. Anyway a smaller package is much easier to carry without attracting attention. I'm going to put it away now."

"Right, I'll arrange things in Frankfurt. I'll let you know tomorrow. I bid you goodnight." Nickolai saw himself out.

Next morning he came back with a plan. Whenever Patrick received the package he was to take it to the Lutheran Church of Saint John in the middle of the city at six o'clock in the evening. If there was a single hymn book on the right of the wide entry step, he was to leave the package on the last pew on the left. When he had done this he was to place two hymn books on the left corner of the step. That would be the end of his involvement.

"I will tell you when the package has been received," said Nickolai.

"And I will tell you when I hear back from Patrick."

He hesitated before he wrote to his son. Of course he was putting him in some danger. But looking at the look of desperation on Nickolai's face, Bertie was beginning to get a faint inkling about what these passports might mean to the right recipients. If there was a problem, Bertie knew he did have sufficient clout to get his son out even if he would have to buy Stanley Baldwin a few drinks. What an imposition!

Bertie took the package to a bookshop he knew well and they readily obliged with a couple of labels and then he went on to meet 'Uncle Frank' at the Spaniards for another lunch. He looked at it. "Doesn't look much but then these things never do." Bertie gave him Patrick's address in Frankfurt and said he was expecting to see his Uncle Frank. Fair enough. Bertie also gave him five hundred pounds in marks, five hundred in sterling and fifty gold sovereigns. "Oh no, this was a favour." "You may need it: these are dangerous times." Echoing Nickolai's warning. "Good Luck."

"I'll let you know when I'm back'." Bertie watched the Fox disappear up the road with the neat little package under his arm. It was a very strange feeling.

On the morning after Nickolai had left for the first time, Bertie asked Joyce whether she still agreed with everything. "You thought I was drunk." He looked a bit sheepish." Yes, you did, you both did. Anyway, I'm fine with what was said, just don't tell me the details."

That was sensible, Bertie thought. There was nothing more he could do now but sit and wait, and have some more ale.

He resumed his normal London life of Parliament, lectures and now increasingly the Athenaeum Club. Sitting in that quiet, rarefied atmosphere, he found it hard to believe that he had been a part of any clandestine action to steal – there was no other word for it – to steal passports and pass them on to… who to? He started laughing: 'You're too old for this, Bertie.' He received a couple of glares. 'Oh sod them' and he ordered another drink.

A couple of weeks later he received a message: 'The Fox has returned to his lair." How ridiculous is this, he felt. Nevertheless he went up to the Spaniards for yet another lunch. It's on me said the Fox. Bertie did not say anything and waited to hear what had happened. The passports had reached Berlin in the Diplomatic Bag and he had picked them up with no problem. Except the atmosphere was so much worse than when he was there a couple of years before: goose stepping, Jews with armbands being insulted. Sadly that was the dominating theme. There was no light relief. But none of it was directed at me, I was treated well. My passport and train tickets were checked firmly but politely and nobody gave the parcel a second glance. I reached Frankfurt and met Patrick. A fine young man."

"Yes, he is." Bertie smiled. "We chatted and he took the parcel as if it were a normal present. He really was cool as a cucumber." Anyway I did not leave him entirely alone. I had a coffee in the cafe across the square and waited to see what he would do."

"That was risky." Bertie said, "for you both."

"I reasoned if it was my son, I'd want somebody to watch his back." "Thanks." said Bertie trying to control his emotions. "Just before six o'clock Patrick left his flat with the parcel under his arm. Again cool as a cucumber. He crossed the street without looking behind him. That's very good in our profession. He rounded the corner into a square. He paused as if he had forgotten something and looked at the church doorstep, I noticed a hymn book on it. Patrick went into the church. Two minutes later he emerged; no package but with a hymn book which he appeared to drop accidentally but then placed on the left of the top entrance step. He added the hymn book from the right and then walked back along the street. No hurrying. He was really nonchalant and then disappeared out of view. I can guarantee no one else followed him.

I stayed with the package. At twenty past six an elderly man walked past the church and glanced at the step. He moved surprisingly quickly into the Church and came out almost immediately with the package. I could not help noticing the look of joy on his face. He looked twenty years younger. He almost ran round the corner in the opposite direction. It did not matter. Nobody noticed him, much less followed him. What the hell was in that parcel?"

"Passports." Bertie replied. "British Passports."

"Whose?... Oh I see, they were blank. Good Lord."

"There were forty." Bertie went on. "There were meant to be a hundred but forty was all they could get in the end."

"A hundred would have been too many to carry: forty was perfect," the Fox said professionally, "the man who picked them

133

up. He was a Jew, wasn't he?"

"Yes probably. I don't know."

"No, I'm sure you don't. Another scheme from one of your constituents."

"Neighbours I have recently discovered actually."

"In my business this is real private enterprise and you pulled it off, Bertie. I would never have thought it. Yes, I really think you pulled it off. Here is the money by the way. I hardly spent any of it."

"No you keep it. You put yourself on the line. You do not know how grateful I am... and a lot of others whose lives you have helped save. They won't know you but you will know. I'd get rid of the marks quickly, they'll be worthless soon. He walked off, deeply moved and immensely proud of his son. He turned to say something to the Fox but he had vanished, melted away.

At the bottom of the chest Alistair found a faded British passport. The official words were familiar but the worried face was not.

20 THE INSPECTOR

Alistair had met some of Bertie's passport holders as a young boy. In the chest there was a folder containing a number of letters both in German and English thanking Bertie. All were heartfelt but a couple stood out. Linking them with Patrick's Journal, Alistair constructed the next part of the story.

The first was written by Sarah Montague, formerly Lewin, the girl who had supplied them to Bertie in the first place. It was a brave letter because it was written while she was still working in the Foreign Office. She described what happened to her father, Solomon Lewin.

Too many prominent Jews were escaping from Frankfurt and the police smelt a rat. Acting on a tip-off, they discovered a Jewish family preparing to go abroad. Inspector Reinhard Schmidt, Gunter's brother, found a blank British passport. He was alone with Solomon, the head of the family. "What is your name?" He asked in English. Solomon looked confused, clearly not understanding the question. "You don't know what I'm talking about, do you. You won't be needing this then, as clearly you do not understand English. I'm afraid I'm taking you into protective custody." Solomon was taken to the Central Police Station and marched into one of the old tiny cells in the basement. In the dim light he could make out lichen on the walls, damp to the touch. He felt utterly alone.

Reinhard was just about to hand in the passport as evidence, but at the last minute he hesitated. He was a man who lived way beyond his means with gambling debts and a liking for expensive prostitutes. This document in his hand was worth a lot to the right person.

He loved the brothels and casinos frowned upon by the Nazis, even they had not managed to close them all down; it was a necessary safety valve as the level of propaganda was stepped up. He pretended to himself and his superiors that he was keeping an eye on the criminals. Some girls offered their services for free but he preferred honest sex for money. Reinhard's wife Magda and their children were totally wrapped up in all the propaganda. He felt he had done his duty in that respect, although all Magda seemed to want was even more children in some insane effort to outpopulate all other races. He was not taken in. He felt that sooner or later, the Nazi dream would crumble. In the First World War he had seen how hard the British and the French had fought. It was fanciful to pretend they had all gone soft or that Germany was as strong as they liked to make you think.

The second letter was from Josef.

And as for the Jews, Reinhard bore them no ill will. He really was just doing his job. But he did have a contact in their camp called Josef; a confidant but also a man to whom he owed a lot of money. He went to see Josef. "Come to pay off your debts?"

"In a manner of speaking. I have come across this." Reinhard showed him the blank passport. "The previous owner was not able to keep his appointment to go abroad on holiday."

"I see."

"Look Josef, I like you but you know how things are. This is not going away. Headquarters are jumping up and down. I am offering you a fair trade. I will give you the passport. In return you can cancel what I owe you and give me half the diamonds you have salted away. If you accept I have to warn you this passport has a short shelf life. They will be very suspicious of all British passports very soon."

"OK Reinhard. I'll go. I appreciate your warning." He went to fetch the diamonds and they divided them fairly. He was just handing over the passport.

"There is one more thing. I need to take something back upstairs.

Who supplied the passports?"

"I believe there is a young English boy living in Frankfurt."

"I see," said Reinhard. Unfortunately he knew exactly who it was.

He drove straight round to Gunter's house. Patrick was present. Luckily Lothar was at a Hitler Youth Candle Vigil. They were all in the middle of dinner but there was no time to save embarrassment. Reinhard addressed the table. He did not reveal the details. Perhaps Patrick had not known himself. After a short time, he tried to leave. "Sit down," said Gunter angrily. Patrick could not have looked more guilty. Anna did not look at all happy either. Perhaps there really is something between them, Reinhard thought, but it's too late for that. He addressed Patrick: "I believe you did not know what got yourself involved in: I'm not interested. I do know your father saved Gunter's life, otherwise I would be arresting you right now. Instead I'm going to drive you round to your flat to get your things and on to the station. There is the midnight train to Basle, arriving in the morning. I will submit my report tomorrow, I will try to keep your name out of it but very soon it will be out of my hands." Patrick looked distraught but he did manage to get up and say. "I am deeply sorry. I was asked to take the package by...by a friend." He turned to leave. Gunter and Greta shook his hand and Anna got up to go with him. Gunter went to stop her but Greta intervened.

Reinhard opened the rear passenger door for Anna and Patrick. It was not far to Patrick's flat and there was plenty of time but there was a traffic hold-up. "Patrick, I should be angry with you. I am really putting myself on the line here."

Patrick was trying to hold Anna's hand but she was having none of it.

They reached his flat. Anna made to get out. "Don't." said Reinhard. Patrick got his things and barely gave the flat a second glance before hurrying back to the car. They reached the station. Anna had thawed and was at least holding his hand now. There was still sufficient time. They went into a bar at the station and Reinhard bought a round of drinks. "Stay here Patrick," he said "I'm off to get..." he paused. They looked up. "Anna, please come with me for a moment."

Reinhard took Anna a couple of tables away and then went to buy the ticket to Basle. When he returned it was time to depart. None of it seemed real but as they said goodbye, Anna clung to him. "You have no idea how much I love you."

He had to get off the train at the border.

"You have been on holiday in the Black Forest." The border guard said in good English as he checked his passport.

"And meeting friends."

"Ah, friends. You must be very careful these days. You never know who your friends are."

Patrick did not know what to make of this. The guard was looking him over, apparently suspecting something. He said nothing. Then he just shrugged, stamped his passport and waved him through. In a few minutes he was in Basle developing a taste for schnapps.

In the chest there was a picture of a classical German blonde smiling by the old Freyhof fountains. She had beautiful eyes. Who would ever forget you?

Josef and his family crossed into France the next day with the last of Bertie's passports.

They never did catch the old man who picked up the package from the church.

Solomon knew he had an appointment. He had been woken up early and given a tiny piece of bread and sausage, just enough to keep going. By 10 o'clock he was ravenous. Surprisingly enough this was exactly when the interrogation began. Reinhard entered the room in a smart uniform that contrasted with the drab prison garb. The inspector appeared to have enjoyed a good breakfast and was deliberately relaxed, as if he was enjoying the meeting. There would be no torture but a few menacing objects lay about the room. Solomon knew it would not be necessary. They would have worked out that he had two children already in Britain. What the inspector would not know was that both of them had key jobs. He was prepared to die but he knew they would not let him if he had something of interest to tell them. He would have to give up one of them. The inspector was sitting in a comfortable chair while Solomon's wrists were already beginning to chafe against his metal restraints.

Reinhard started with the daughter, pretending to know more than he did. Solomon tried to deny it but that did not last long. "So she works for the government, what department?" Solomon very nearly said Foreign Office but luckily at the last moment managed to say "Ministry of Pensions." Not quite believing him, Reinhard thought he would change tack and go for the son. He must have enlisted by now.

"What service has he joined?"

"The army," was his first answer, but Reinhard had his measure now and decided to exert the simple pressure of silence; it worked.

"The RAF." Solomon said at last, and then it all came out. He was not a pilot but he was in the new bomber command HQ – this was getting very interesting. In the early afternoon, the deal was struck: if his son cooperated, Solomon's life would be saved and he could live under house arrest. This would last as long as his son continued to provide information. Subtle pressure was applied by embassy staff in London, and the Germans got a mole in the RAF.

His sister's role in the foreign office remained undiscovered.

Bertie was at the bar in the Spaniards again after a hospital meeting. Picking a quiet moment, Peter said. "Two gentleman came in the pub asking after you."

"What did you tell them?"

"I said you were a salesman from up North."

"That just about covers it." Said Bertie. "What was I supposed to be selling?"

"Hair Products." Peter replied, without sarcasm.

"Thanks a lot! I suppose they fell for that one."

"One of them wrote it down in his notebook."

21 THE FRIAR AND THE TRAMP

The older children understood that this would probably be the last summer at Beech Court – Lily had decided to sell up and retire anyway, the uncertain future was damaging parents' confidence – Walmer was now no place for a girl's boarding school, there was talk of requisition and evacuation. Patrick and CJ were now both far too old for summer school but Bertie and Joyce were both very busy at home. Lily always had a soft spot for Patrick and recognised that his parent's preoccupations were not good for him. That summer Patrick seemed particularly distant. Lily had seen a lot in her 20 years as headmistress and could read the signs. She invented a pretext to get him on his own, helping out in her study.

Unknown to Lily a child was secretly eavesdropping behind the curtain. A fragment describing this encounter was in the same handwriting that recounted Lothar's visit.

"How did your trip to Germany go, Patrick?" She asked gently. "Oh, it was great ...." he started, but was aware of Lily staring straight at him. He stopped for a moment. "Can I talk to you in confidence?"

"Please do, I hoped you would." She sat down in her leather chair, motioning Patrick to the seat across the desk.

"What is said in this room, stays in this room." Lily said, unaware of the presence of their companion.

"I don't know where to start. Gunter was as good as his word and I got a brilliant job and a flat. His family invited me round all the time, especially on Sundays. Lothar tried to recruit me into the Hitler Youth."

"A bit more spicy than the Walmer war club?"

"Oh yes, I did go once but that was quite enough, though I see it would be different if I was German."

"That's sad – and what about his sister?"

"Oh, Anna and I were ... very good friends."

Lily was very sharp. "You love her?"

"Yes....I just don't know."

"But she loves you?"

"Yes, I think she does."

"You feel you should be there for her?"

"Yes I do." Patrick brightened up a little at Lily's understanding. "But something happened?" Lily asked, and he told her a bit about the parcel and the reaction from Gunter's brother. Lily put her arm round him. "I'm very sorry Patrick, I think everything's all out of our hands now, just keep writing to Anna." And the tiny Lily took the much taller Patrick out to have a cup of tea. Afterwards she went back into the study and looked out of the window. She told herself she would miss this place and this view. Emma had been telling her about all the Jewish refugees settling around Hampstead and Golders Green. Bertie, you old devil, I really wouldn't put it past you!

The friar and the tramp walked past the German Embassy in Chesham Place and looked through the window. There was feverish activity inside as the staff packed up and burned documents. A uniformed man with a swastika glared at them. They moved on past an empty garage. The splendid staff car had long gone and Ribbentrop with it. He had become German Foreign Minister and had signed a pact with Molotov, his Soviet opposite number. Surprisingly friendly by all accounts; consummate professionals.

This time there would be no waving of pieces of paper. Britain was going to war as Germany invaded Poland in a dispute over Danzig, now Gdansk, then a free city the British Public knew even less about than Czechslovakia. Nonetheless Patrick and CJ had both been called up and the family decided to say goodbye at home. As they had both served in the school Cadet Corps, they were eligible to become officers immediately. CJ went off to Sandhurst for a short course before accepting a commission with the South Notts. Patrick, somewhat following his father, joined up as a private and was told to report to Shrewsbury on September 3rd, the day war was declared. He decided to walk to the station.

He felt utterly dejected. The letters from Anna had dried up, there would be no more now. His ideals about the League of Nations had been shattered. The Spanish Republic had been extinguished and now he was preparing to fight against Anna's country. He felt he probably would still be there if he had not abused the family hospitality.

Deep in thought, he barely noticed two figures beside him, a friar and a tramp. On the face of it they were an unlikely couple but they kept a respectful silence. Patrick woke out of his reverie and offered to buy them a cup of tea. The tramp was very ready to accept cash but the friar replied in a dignified way that they would only accept if Patrick joined them.

They found a cafe and Patrick ordered three lunches. The tramp looked as if he had not had a good meal for a long time. He told Patrick about the German Embassy as he wolfed down his food. Afterwards he soon fell asleep in the warm atmosphere.

Father Algy was an Anglican Franciscan friar who chose to exercise his ministry among the itinerant community. But he was a remarkable priest and he let Patrick tell his story. Algy had a quietness about him which touched Patrick deeply. In the end he broke down and cried. Algy prayed in the silence that followed, it seemed wholly appropriate. At last he said to Patrick. "You cannot know if you'll ever see Anna again. Everything is possible. I do not know why your father asked you to deliver the parcel but I am sure it must have been of great significance. I am also sure that both Anna and your father will want you to survive, and I, too, will pray for you. You will find friends."

The tramp woke up and he and Algy thanked Patrick for the meal and departed on their walk to the next spike. Patrick got to the station and caught the train to Shrewsbury, along with hundreds of children being evacuated. There was just time to sign in at the barracks. He was told to report back the next day. He wandered about the town aimlessly and ended up in the Abbey in the early evening. Once a place of sanctuary, that was exactly what he did not find. He was sitting on a pew in the middle of the nave, utterly drained of any purpose or even will to live. He did not know how long he sat there but a gentle voice asked him if he was alright. Patrick said he was but the speaker could see that was far from the case and invited him to take supper with him. Patrick accepted weakly. The stranger took him back to his home and his wife prepared an extra place.

Patrick thawed a little during the meal and found it impossible to resist the offer of a bed, into which he sank and slept until late the next morning. The man had left but his wife insisted he have a full breakfast – he had to report to the barracks at midday. He never did get round to thanking the stranger.

In common with millions of other families, Joyce and Bertie found themselves with a house empty of children for the first time in 20 years. Not ones for showing tremendous outward affection there was a huge hole in their lives, to which neither would admit to themselves, let alone the other. Bertie felt so guilty and helpless as he was pulled along by events which were now totally out of his control. There was Chamberlain's new War Ministry but Labour and Bertie were left kicking their heels. As the weeks went on, life returned to some degree of normality, Bertie resumed taking evening classes, which were well attended. Bertie and Joyce received welcome post from Patrick and CJ. A man from the Ministry of Health arrived at the Manor House Hospital demanding the immediate requisition of 200 beds for emergency cover for air raid casualties. He wanted to move all patients out there and then. Ambrose demanded to see his authority. He blustered but could not produce any. Luckily he never returned. Above all, perhaps, the dreaded mass air raids did not materialise immediately and with so many having been evacuated, London seemed strangely quiet.

Both Patrick and CJ had been posted to the new BEF in Northern France which was getting stronger by the day. Patrick was now driving a brand new Bedford truck which he loved. The crew had adopted an Alsatian, dog not person, or rather she had adopted them. The dog growled ferociously when anybody unauthorised came anywhere near the lorry. They called her Bella, and from day one she was Patrick's dog. They all shared their rations and Bella was not above bringing the odd chicken to the party, no questions asked.

Bertie remembered how depressed he had been over the death of Wilfred Owen, who still stared at him from the frame on his desk. What did you die for? He went down into the chamber. There was yet another fruitless protest debate about the inadequacies of the Allied response to the German invasion of Norway. Bertie had been here before. The debate was winding up predictably. He knew the signs.

Then Lloyd George, who had been in the House for fifty years but now led just a handful of MPs, stood up. He waited until the House was quiet and then proceeded to demolish the Prime Minister and in ten minutes single-handedly changed the course of the war. Bertie listened with growing admiration as Chamberlain, no mean parliamentary performer himself, visibly shrank and began to look very ill.

It was the best opposition speech he had ever heard by far. If only the tables had been turned, he thought, and it had been Lloyd George he had destroyed, not the Secretary of State for War, what could have happened then? But he hadn't and neither had any of the other pacifist MPs in World War One. Maybe he had come the closest.

A couple of days later, Bertie was having a drink in the bar. At least this was still functioning, he thought. Churchill had become Prime Minister and exuded a confidence that Chamberlain never possessed. However there were disturbing rumours from the continent.

'I know where he'll be.' Churchill went to the House of Commons Bar. There was a rather drunken cheer. He went over to Bertie who stood up and offered his hand in congratulation. "I will take your hand if you join me and accept the post of Leader of the Opposition."

Bertie was absolutely astonished. But he managed to reply.

"Don't worry, I won't give you much trouble."

"No, I hope you will. You are the leader of the Labour party whilst Clement Atlee and the rest are otherwise engaged. Well done."

"You too," said Bertie, but Churchill had swept on.

Joyce will be pleased, he thought, though it would mean they would spend even less time together.

Stanley Baldwin congratulated him and presented an inscribed solid silver hip flask. "Fill it with good Port." He said. "Very generous of you. But isn't this part of a ploy to wheedle information from unwitting members of the Coalition?" "It's worked well before," replied Stanley.

Alistair looked at the flask. Indeed it had been a generous gift. 'To our Friendship' the inscription read.

22 THE TRAP

The next month presented perhaps the worst situation that any new British prime minister has ever had to face. Now in the centre of government, Bertie watched the situation deteriorate by the day.

Alistair followed his journals and the diaries of Patrick and CJ, both now in the BEF across the channel. The debacle in Norway is rapidly followed by almost simultaneous German invasions of France, Holland, Denmark and Belgium. It's neutrality smashed, the allies rushed the French Strategic reserve and the BEF into Flanders, as in WW1.

The order came for Patrick's lorry to cross the frontier into Belgium. They were yet to see a German, let alone fight one, but as they travelled east the roads began to fill up with refugees heading in the opposite direction. They reached their objective on the river Dyle. It was still very quiet with no evidence of the enemy.

However, in a couple of days there was a concentrated German break-through in the lightly defended area of the Ardennes to the south. Panzers managed to cross the river Meuse in numbers, despite desperate attempts to blow up the bridge by the RAF who suffered the worst losses in their history. Bertie soon realised this was a very different war from the last. The British managed a counter attack. It was not coordinated with the French, but a British shell still managed to kill the German Chief of Staff. Rommel, standing immediately next to him, was badly shaken but not even scratched.

CJ was in his element as a junior officer and had already been promoted to Captain. He was now leading his platoon in a fighting retreat through Belgium. They came to the site of Le Cateau, the World War I battlefield, the last battle to begin and end in one day.

We will be lucky to last until lunchtime, CJ thought, as he chose his defensive position, not far from the cemetery full of white gravestones that gleamed in the sun and could have been laid yesterday. The Germans did not expect any resistance so after the initial exchange of fire there was a lull while they brought up reinforcements; CJ was on his own. Suddenly a Hurricane flew low in between the British and German lines. It was on fire and CJ could see the pilot desperately trying to extinguish the flames. He made a crash landing 200 yards away, just next to the cemetery. CJ immediately put up a white flag and rushed towards the stricken plane with two of his men. This was respected and German soldiers also ran towards the plane to attempt a rescue. Through the flames they could see the pilot slide back the cockpit canopy. Just then a dark figure emerged very quickly from the graveyard and appeared to lift the pilot out. The flames died down but it was still very smoky; CJ and the Germans arrived at the plane almost simultaneously. The pilot was propped up against a gravestone, although his uniform and face were unmarked. He managed to gasp the words "Granville-Mathers" before he died. CJ looked in his uniform, that was the name on the warrant card. He was laying the man flat on the ground when he noticed the name on the gravestone was also Granville-Mathers; it must have been his father trying to rescue him and bring him to rest, CJ thought. The German officer said. "He has passed away, ja?"

"Yes, I will give him a quick burial service." CJ replied.

"We have a Pastor." The officer said. "We will take the service together." So CJ and the Lutheran pastor stood side by side through the short service. It was the first funeral CJ ever took and he never forgot it. "I think you are heading for the coast now, we will give you half an hour." The German officer said as he saluted.

Rommel pressed on to take Rheims and head for the channel ports. The nightmare scenario that the trenches of the First World War had managed to prevent for four years was now happening within days. A British army of 300,000 men, including Bertie's sons, Patrick and Christopher, were trapped in Belgium. Luckily the British commander, Lord Gort, out of touch with London and against written orders, believed the intelligence reports he received from Hut 6, Blecthley Park and ordered a retreat to Dunkirk - a fighting retreat in the midst of a flow of 12 million refugees.

Orders came through for Patrick's lorry to go north. Progress was slightly easier as most of the refugees were heading west. They were still at least 100 miles from the coast, which, although nobody said as much, would be their destination. They settled down for the night at a small crossroads, camping out behind a hedge. It had begun to rain which further dampened their spirits. A mist added to the depressing atmosphere. At 4am Bella woke Patrick up. He thought someone was trying to get into the lorry but then he heard a low diesel sound – he immediately recognised German engines. He woke the others; there was nothing they could do but lie low and stay quiet, even Bella seemed to realise the need for absolute silence. A group of 10 tanks passed by them heading west but failed to see them. Patrick thought he recognised the officer in the lead tank but was too tired to process the information. After the tanks passed the group rapidly resumed their drive north before they could be caught by the following infantry.

There was to be no Agincourt. Again interpreting the intelligence reports from Hut 6, the Navy ordered every available craft over thirty feet to assemble at the English Channel ports to prepare for possible evacuation. Luckily again, another naval officer with an eye for detail, realised that large numbers of troops could best be moved out of Dunkirk by using a narrow mole jutting a mile out to sea.

 En route to the coast, Patrick noticed that Bella was quiet, almost pensive. When they reached the coast they were diverted to Dunkirk as Calais and Boulogne were already cut off. Close to the beach was a truck graveyard where they were directed to take their kit and disable the lorry, putting it beyond further use. Bella had disappeared; Patrick thought she had run away but she was at the back of the lorry and would not leave. There was not much time – Patrick realised she would not leave him or the lorry, despite his best efforts. Desperately and with shaking hands, he got out his revolver and shot her. He felt as badly as he had ever done.

There was no time for reflection as they were shepherded on to the beach where a surreal scene awaited them. Tens of thousands of soldiers were spread across the huge expanse of dunes. There were frequent attacks by German aircraft but Patrick noticed that although terrifying, they were often less effective than he would have thought, as many of the bombs exploded harmlessly deep in the sand. The group stood in file – the Royal Navy Beachmaster was directing the line with the authority of a headmaster taking a roll call, completely oblivious of all that was going on around him. He inspired confidence. As Patrick got nearer he could see the long narrow mole stretching almost out of sight. Larger ships were moored alongside, picking up troops, while much smaller craft picked up men from the foreshore. He got on to the mole and realised how long it was. Of course, the Germans tried to bomb it but as it was a very thin target, bombs exploded in the sea, throwing up mountains of spray. Drenched but still alive, Patrick reached the point of departure.

The next ship on the mole was the paddle steamer, Pride of Brodick. Although Patrick was exhausted, he noticed that the original peacetime crew were still manning the ship under its captain and a Naval Commander. There was an orderly queue and hundreds of soldiers including Patrick embarked rapidly, finding a place to stand on deck. Two destroyers were on guard out at sea. The Pride of Brodick set off slowly from the mole. There was another ship waiting to replace it. A Stuka flew towards them. The ship had not built up any momentum but one of the destroyers saw what was happening and moved between the ship and the Stuka, putting up a tremendous volume of fire. The other destroyer created a protective screen of smoke out to sea. The pilot was going for the obvious target of the paddle steamer. It reminded Patrick of happier times with Anna on ships steaming up the Rhine. The pilot forced himself to press home the attack but the curtain of fire was too much so he diverted to one of the destroyers. The captain was too agile for him and the bomb missed narrowly, throwing up a huge wall of spray. The Pride of Brodick escaped into open water and under the smoke screen. It could only have lasted a couple of minutes but Patrick knew the courage and seamanship of the navy and the volunteers had saved his life.

The boat jolted as it reached Ramsgate; Patrick woke up with a start, not knowing where he was – he was incredibly stiff but he shook himself and looked out of a porthole at the harbour full of craft. Everybody was being moved off at the double so the ship could return to Dunkirk as soon as possible. On shore it was chaotic. Patrick gave his name and number . "Are we in England?" He checked.

"Yes of course, just to prove it here is a nice cup of tea and a sandwich, they don't do that for you in Germany!" It was just such a welcoming atmosphere as they hung around waiting. The army did not seem to be expecting anybody to make it back from France. Eventually they were told to board a lorry and he fell asleep again as it moved off. He woke up just as they turned into Beech Court. They were assigned beds in the old familiar dormitories – it felt like coming home. Patrick slept more peacefully than he had for a long time. The next morning they were woken up at 9 but Patrick had got up much earlier and had taken a walk round his old haunts. He found the place where Harold had received his fatal arrow wound and the little rise in the ground where Custer had made his last stand. Blucher will not be relieving us today, he thought.

But the bridgehead still had to be defended.

CJ reached Dunkirk, but his battle was not over; he was tasked with fighting a rearguard action to try to hold off the German tanks, using the natural obstacle of the Albert canal. This was a good idea on paper, CJ thought, but the land was totally flat and there was very little cover. However, there was a lot of abandoned equipment of various sorts and even a lot of food. Still CJ did not rate his chances of holding out against determined attack as very high. On the first day they dug in at the two bridges that crossed the canal. CJ thought that whichever bridge the Germans went for they could concentrate their fire on the tanks and then destroy the bridge at the last minute. In the event it stayed quiet all day, there was no attack. Unknown to CJ, the German High Command had ordered a rest day for all their tanks, overriding the advice of local commanders.

The King of Belgium kept the German officers waiting. He realised he had been duped into declaring war at the last minute and thus had dragged the now doomed BEF and the French Reserve into his country. He looked out into the courtyard and realised that the Germans wanted his surrender to be as amicable as possible so he thought he would play their game. Everybody stood to attention as he entered the room and engaged in polite conversation. After an hour he said he suddenly felt unwell and retired, not to be seen again that day. The Allies had got another 24 hours.

The third day was different altogether. A ceasefire had been concluded with the Belgians and the Germans turned their attention to the trapped British and French armies. In the morning some tanks attacked the bridge on CJs left side and were repulsed with difficulty. During the respite, CJ withdrew the guns over the bridge. Some German tanks stormed across the bridge and formed up to attack. The bridge was mined, CJ had hoped that he could blow up a German tank as it was crossing but the detonator jammed and the Germans got across. CJ could retreat no further. The tanks advanced and the British guns were firing open breach. In the midst of the fighting one of his gunners stood up and saluted, saying "Permission to remove my teeth, Sir." "Permission granted." The leading tank got nearer and they managed to knock one of the tracks. It veered over the left and blocked the other tanks. CJ thought what a lucky shot that was. In the short lull, he led a small party along the towpath, mostly out of view of the tanks, and managed to ignite the charge and blow up the bridge; it was a very close thing. They retreated to the other crossing that the Germans must now use. The few German tanks on the British side of the canal did not follow them. No heroics this time, thought CJ, we'll blow it up as soon as they get close. Although they came under some strafing fire from a bomber, the second German attack did not come until early evening. Through his binoculars CJ could see at least 50 tanks approaching in good formation, it was time to go. He blew up the bridge and began the long march back to Dunkirk – they were evacuated later that night.

Meanwhile the cabinet was on a knife edge. Sometimes included for key votes and sometimes not, Bertie fully supported Churchill against the serious moves for a negotiated settlement with Hitler. In this war, Stanley and Bertie stood together for the Coalition, it was Bertie's turn to keep Stanley in the loop. Churchill's hand steadily strengthened as over nine days the British army was evacuated from Dunkirk.

It would now all rest on the outcome of the Battle of Britain.

The family dragged Bertie off for a celebratory meal. Joyce was so proud of her sons. They had grown up so well. They all realised how fragile life was and the importance of appreciating what they had.

A rather high pitched, plummy, but articulate and calm voice, crackled over the radio as Anthony Eden addressed the nation, announcing the formation of a Home Defence Force. There was no rhetoric, call to duty or flummery - there did not need to be. Hundreds of men were trying to sign up before the short broadcast had even finished, followed by hundreds of thousands in the next few weeks. He had struck exactly the right chord.

John Dyer was sitting outside a pub just off the Old Kent Road savouring a beer on the lovely summer evening. He was so proud. In his hand there were the latest directives from Labour HQ in

Transport House signed by Bertie. He felt so honoured to have served with him and incredibly glad he had managed to rescue him on the Somme. He was listening to the broadcast through the window. He would join up when he finished his pint. His attention was caught by a column of soldiers marching purposefully down the Old Kent Road towards Dover. The light was fading but he swore he could make out First World War puttees. It definitely was not the beer. It had been watered down months ago.

23 OLYMPIA

Just how close Bertie had come to the centre of power became dramatically clear a couple of weeks later. One evening a large staff car drove up to his house; two officers got out and knocked on the front door. Bertie opened it and his first thought was that there had been a military coup. Both officers were unsmiling.

"You have to come with us, Sir." Bertie got his hat. There was no conversation. They were driving north. They arrived at Olympia station where there was a small reception party.

"This way, Sir." If it was a coup this was an odd place to be brought to, or was there some huge holding area in the exhibition centre? He was ushered into the main hall but instead of a prison there were a lot of temporary desks and seating. A quiet air of determination and sense of purpose prevailed. In the distance he could see cabinet colleagues. He was just thinking about going across when a young RAF officer approached him, saluted, smiled and asked Bertie to follow him, this time courteously.

"I expect you are wondering why you are here. Sir."

"Please call me Bertie, I am uncomfortable enough already."

"I am sorry but you will understand the need for all this in a moment." They sat down at a desk. "Bertie, what I am about to tell you is top secret and not to be divulged to anybody and I must ask you to sign this." A document headed DEFENCE OF THE REALM ACT was thrust in front of him. I am too old for this, thought Bertie, but he decided not to question the legality, questions would be for later. He signed the paper and passed it over and sat back before asking the young man to continue.

"The German bombers fly across the Channel, escorted by fighters. Most enemy formations can be seen out at sea with the help of radar before they cross our shores. This gives fighter command enough time to scramble Hurricanes and Spitfires, get them off the ground and fly them to the right height in place to meet the oncoming planes. There is an army of Observer Corps to track the formations when they reach land. But the whole thing depends on a fully functioning telephone network. A telephone system I helped to protect and extend, mused Bertie. "Radar gives vital extra minutes, the Germans have been knocking out our radar but the masts are usually replaced rapidly so cover is still pretty good. This afternoon a lucky bomb hit the telephone exchange of the main Biggin Hill command centre. The estimates are it will be down for at least a week. The only alternative is the army of motor cycle despatch riders we are now using like never before."

"You say usually." Bertie said.

"Yes, you're right, the radar cover is also significantly down. Our main forward airfields are really badly damaged. The aircraft are being replaced but the pilots ..." he paused – Bertie sensed he was talking about friends. "The pilots are not." Bertie was already aware of most of what he had just heard. Then the Officer did surprise him.

"That is not the key problem. We have intelligence reports that the crack German Parachute Division is preparing to take over key airfields for long enough to enable an invasion to take place by air. In that event the government is dispersed immediately to carry on the battle from the British heartland. That is why you are here." That would never work, thought Bertie. He said aloud. "Where am I being sent to?"

"I cannot tell you that." Bertie could guess.

"We are waiting for the final orders from Churchill."

"Why here?"

"Oh I can tell you that - Olympia is the heart of the railway network."

They all went home the next morning. The Germans never took the airfields; the Post Office worked round the clock to repair the exchange in three days; there was persistent low cloud over Southern England. Intelligence could not have known that General Student, the key architect of parachute assault, had been seriously wounded by a stray bullet during the occupation of Antwerp. The Germans switched their target to London.

Bertie had been tasked with going round the country to assess Army morale. He demanded, and got, Patrick as driver. It was a special time for them both. A few weeks later they were on Hampstead Heath watching the German bombers still in formation. Apparently they had got through. The few RAF planes seemed easily brushed aside by the fighter escorts. "This is the last throw, you know." said Bertie.

"Look over there." Patrick pointed.

"Fantastic!" They were both overwhelmed with pride as a big wing of sixty Hurricanes flew in from the north and joined in the fight. London was saved.

They both cheered. After a while, Bertie turned to Patrick and said. "Look, I admire you for not immediately taking a commission. It's what I did myself. You've seen what life is it like for the ordinary Tommy. But now I think you should consider becoming an officer. I'm so proud of you." "Oh, I'm just doing my duty. I haven't been doing anything special."

"Actually I meant delivering the package in Frankfurt." Patrick looked at his father. They sat down on a bench. Patrick told him about the policeman and the trip to Basle. He paused. "I wanted to marry Anna." "I'm really sorry." Said Bertie quietly. "Perhaps it will happen."

They both knew how unlikely that was.

Despite himself, Patrick was promoted to 2nd lieutenant. However, he still got to drive around on his beloved brand new Triumph, lovingly maintained by his Corporal, and found every excuse to drive it as much as possible. Orders came through for him to report with bike to a camp near Aldeburgh on the Norfolk coast. It was well over 100 miles away, needing an almost full tank of petrol. The next day he bade farewell to his unit and began the drive to East Anglia. It started to rain almost immediately; although he had a large motorbike cape the water soon began to penetrate. As he rode east, the ground got flatter and more exposed, the rain horizontal, as only it can be in East Anglia. The visibility was blurred by condensation inside his goggles. The main A12 was not difficult to follow despite all the road signs having been removed, but eventually he had to take minor roads to Aldeburgh and the coast and got thoroughly lost as well as soaked through. Eventually he reached his destination, it was almost dark. Instead of a nice welcoming cup of tea the sergeant shouted. "You're late, the chief is very angry."

"I know, I got lost in the driving rain." "Tell that to the Chief, he's heard it all before. He wants to see you right now." The sergeant took Patrick to the chief's office almost at a run; he opened the door and Patrick burst in, saluting "I'm sorry I'm late sir. I..." and then he looked down at his new Commanding Officer, who was beside himself with laughter, as was the sergeant standing behind Patrick.

"My God, it's you." said Patrick, staring down at his brother. Patrick had always been senior, but not now. Over the next few weeks, as Patrick saw how well CJ actually did his job he found a new respect for him.

CJ did tend to see the larger picture. He was in command of 20 miles of coast at high risk of invasion. He decided to fortify the local church tower as it had the best view for miles around. When the unit had finished its work, CJ and Patrick were standing on the roof looking out on a magnificent sunset, casting huge shadows over to the river estuary. It was so peaceful, CJ found it really uplifting, relishing the silence. After a while Patrick said. "The lead on this roof must be worth at least £400." 'Oh dear,' thought CJ.

The smoking Spitfire came down on the parade ground, perhaps the pilot thought it was an airfield, or just did not have much choice. He did not land well and the plane immediately burst into flames. The pilot struggled to pull open the canopy but to no avail. Patrick was the nearest and led a team trying to rescue him; the flames were too intense but they did not sufficiently obscure the spectacle of the pilot desperately struggling to get out - his dying screams stayed with them.

About a week later, a car pulled up at the base and a man in a grey suit stepped out. With quiet firmness the man from the Ministry insisted on seeing the commander. CJ received him politely with a cup of tea. The man took out a form from his briefcase and passed it to CJ. He read through the officialease and reached the nub. "You cannot be serious." He said.

"No, I am. The church is consecrated ground and therefore cannot be used for military purposes."

"But it dominates the whole estuary and is within the two mile military exclusion zone." CJ replied.

"No, it's 100 yards outside and therefore subject to civilian rules. "

"And if there is an invasion?"

"Then you will have to apply to rescind the order."

As if we'd have time, thought CJ, but he realised he would have to comply, or at least appear to. "Thank you for bringing this to my attention, we will do it immediately."

They did dismantle the fortifications, or at least some of them, leaving enough so they could be reconstructed quickly. It gave CJ an idea. He called Patrick into his office and they got out some maps, poring over them. Someone took a photo of the group.

After his experiences on the Albert canal, CJ was critically aware of the power of German tanks. If I was a tank commander, deciding where to invade, East Anglia would be an excellent choice because it is so flat and there are no obstacles, he mused. As he travelled round his command he had noticed a dyke, and then another, then yet another – there were hundreds of them, all to hold back water, water that would prevent the passage of tanks.

So, age 19, he ordered all the dykes to be raised and vast areas of hinterland went under water. There never was any invasion by German tanks, even had it ever been seriously considered.

The orders came through for Patrick to depart to the Eighth Army in North Africa as a Captain in the Supply Corps.

There was a photo of the family saying goodbye on a platform. It was a press photo but intrusive and certainly not posed like the studio portraits. Alistair supposed it had been a paparazzi shot. Bertie and Joyce were there and CJ had taken leave to be there. They could almost be having a hug. On the back Joyce had written: Last Time Together.

Next year in the spring, the threat of German Land invasion diminished as Hitler turned his armies east to invade Russia. The RAF maintained its radar vigilance especially on clear sunny days. On one such morning a new radar operator noticed blips on the shimmering cathode ray screen. He called his supervisor. A more experienced colleague said. "It's just birds."

"Don't be ridiculous they're far too small to show up."

"Not if they fly together in large numbers." Anyway the alarm was raised and a platoon sent to investigate. They drove through the flat fens to a seawall that offered some view of the coast. The sea was now a mile away across tidal mud flats. This was the result of the lifting of the dykes the previous year. It was low tide and the main feature of the scene was ooze and mud. CJ shivered. He got out his binoculars and saw there had been an invasion... of hundreds of thousands of wading birds from the occupied continent, choosing the new site to stock up on their annual journey north.

24 THE SQUASHED HAT

Alistair picked up Sarah Montagu's letter.

She was sorting some files at the back of the minister's office in the Foreign Office. The Permanent Secretary walked in. Eden was writing furiously at his desk but stopped and looked up. "You are early," he said.

"It's another no-go at the embassy I'm afraid." The perm sec replied. "The Russians still believe our warnings of invasion are part of a capitalist plot."

"If only that were the case," said Eden gloomily. "Of course we need them, now more than ever."

"This just might interest you, sir," said the perm sec. "Our agents are in a position to mount a coup in Belgrade."

"That would be excellent, the Germans could hardly ignore the threat on their southern flank, it would delay them for at least a couple of weeks." said Eden.

"Which might take them into the winter in Russia." The perm sec said presciently. "A kind of Sarejevo in reverse."

"The revenge of the Hapsburgs." Eden rejoined. "They would make our job a lot easier." Sarah looked at the large map of Europe on the wall in front of her; there was a dotted line stretching 2,500 miles from north of Finland to the Black Sea denoting the borders of Germany and its allies. Could Hitler really be thinking of invading Russia?

If Inspector Reinhart Schmidt had discovered Solomon's daughter worked in the Foreign Office and recruited her as a spy this would be the intelligence coup of the century. Solomon had made the right choice in giving up his son to the Germans.

Eden rose with his memo in hand and told the perm sec. "Do not commit anything to writing."

Just up the road, Bertie had left his hat in the bar of the House of Commons after an evening drink. He was getting increasingly forgetful these days. Annoyed with himself, he took the tube to Westminster. It was a pleasant spring morning. He walked into Parliament Square. It had gone. All was eerily quiet. He looked round in shock. It had not entirely gone but was almost unrecognisable. St Pauls might have been saved but the Luftwaffe had hit the House of Commons. At least no one had been hurt. A single policeman stood guard. He managed to walk round to the terrace next to the Thames. There was a lot of fallen masonry but the part nearest to the river was largely unaffected, there was still a lone chair where he and Gunter had had a drink only a couple of years before. You were right, my friend and now you have bought the Reichstag fire to us – I think we will survive however; and even our democracy, after the war. He made his way into the ruined bar. There was his hat from Liberty's, fatally flattened. He walked back out, hat under arm. Someone was auctioning off remnants of stone. He bought a Tudor Rose. Life went on.

He never got round to buying a new hat. The squashed hat was neatly laid out in a box in the chest. Alistair looked out of the window. The heron had moved onto the stone from the House of Commons, now a proud part of the rockery.

Bertie had never been so busy, keeping the Labour party going, life blood of Britain, he thought, along with the unions and shop stewards. He thought of his trip to the USA, They were now fighting alongside us. He had done his bit, did they really need him anymore, surely they could get someone else. He hardly spent any time with Joyce. Perhaps he really had been too old for her. She too had never been busier with her war work. She was now in her element, a leading figure in the London Womans Voluntary Service; she also looked superb, really looking after herself. He stopped himself thinking any further.

Their sons were gone of course, brave young men both of them in different ways and CJ was now the youngest Colonel in the British Army. Anyway, they must spend more time together, he would make time. He could make up an official trip somewhere nice, they owed him that, he could swing it. The Labour party in St Ives was definitely in need of a visit.

To Bertie's surprise, Molotov met everybody personally. "So, you are the Leader of the Opposition, a German spy," he said mischieviously.

"Well, it was you who met Ribbentrop."

"I cannot deny it, it's strange how our names will be linked forever and that is the only thing people will remember us for." Yes, strange indeed, Bertie thought afterwards, to be remembered for just one thing. It's still the manifesto, better than nothing I suppose. All his support for Russia in the early years, then feeling used by Russians 'as a front', now friends and allies again, had they really changed or was it all the consequence of Hitler's incredible decision to invade? Bertie looked at the cold, clear, grey but impressive eyes and thought of all the purges, the labour camps and executions. He felt relieved he was in London and not Moscow. They smiled and shook hands.

It was a clear night and the radar had picked up a lot of enemy activity; they had decoded some Luftwaffe messages and anyway it was obvious that the target was going to be London. The London Fire Brigade HQ summoned as much help from outside the capital as it could.

A smartly dressed Russian officer walked over to Molotov, saluted and gave him a message. He said to Bertie. "There is an air raid warning but I'm not going anywhere."

Bertie said. "Are you sure about that, Sir?"

Molotov faced him and replied. "Let me tell you a story: a couple of months ago I was in Moscow; we could hear artillery and

German tanks had reached the metro system – there was complete panic in the city. Nevertheless, there was an orderly evacuation of key factories. Some ministries had already been moved eastwards beyond the Urals. The Politbureau was standing on the main station awaiting their turn. The station clock had stopped. The shells seemed very close. The train stopped at the platform. Nobody moved. Stalin raised his head and began to pace up and down. There was total silence and the shelling seemed to stop. He continued pacing for what seemed like a very long time but can only have been several minutes. He then turned to face us and said. "We're not going anywhere - we are staying here." So the whole evacuation of Moscow was abandoned. The Germans have advanced no further and we're still there. That is why I am not going into the air raid shelter."

"We ourselves have been very close to evacuating London," said Bertie quietly.

"I bet Churchill paced up and down one of your platforms." replied Molotov. "But you, my friend, must leave the embassy now, otherwise you will have to stay here in the basement: 'Leader of the Opposition defects to the Russians.' That's a good headline for your Evening Standard."

"Protective custody?" Bertie replied.

"Yes, that's what we used to call it," and they shook hands again.

Bertie did not go home immediately, as Molotov had prompted him. He was close to the offices of the Evening Standard, his old newspaper, and walked in on a whim. He went up to the newsroom, tick-a-tape was coming in of a serious Japanese breakthrough in the battle for Hong Kong harbour. There had been a bombing raid by the RAF on Scharnhorst and Gneisenau in Brest harbour. Hong Kong would soon fall. Bertie read an account of the last ship out. It was being meticulously loaded by hand. The Captain noticed a Japanese Officer walk around the hill overlooking the harbour. It was time to go. The mate made the coolies load the remaining boxes before they fled. They were just about to raise the gangplank when the Captain noticed a lone carved chest on the wharf. "Too good for the Japs," said the Captain and he ordered a couple of his astonished crew to carry it on board. The chest began the long journey to Britain.

Bertie had had enough; he turned round, went out and waited for a bus home – it was freezing. The bombing raid did not seem to have materialised. Eventually the bus came and then he walked back up the hill from Golders Green, sans hat - he was cold and exhausted.

Bertie decided to take one of his long baths. He got his journal right up to date while waiting for the water to hot up. There was a flat black line at the bottom of the page. He was being called. He got into the water and relaxed. He mused how the war would be won now the USA and Russia were fighting on Britain's side, he was so glad about Russia. This bath is so nice and hot – he leaned across to pick up some soap. There was no time to cry out as a massive wall of pain hit him in his chest for a couple of seconds just before there was total blackness.

25 THE WAKE

Joyce cautiously opened the bathroom door. "Bertie." She said softly, but she knew there would be no reply. He was facing the wall, so she was addressing the back of his head; this is how I first met you, she thought irreverently. She supposed she had always known this might happen one day, particularly since the king's funeral. But there could be no preparation, even if she had been that way inclined, which she certainly never was. She just wanted to be alone with him, she had thought he might still be around for a while. Anyway, the all-clear had not yet sounded and she did not want to put others at risk unnecessarily. She closed his eyes, went downstairs and poured herself a strong drink. It tasted very good – she knew what to do – they had been very clear, day or night. She rang the number, a senior official answered her immediately; he was very sympathetic and understanding. "Just stay where you are, we will be there very shortly. We will contact your son now." There was a pause. "I want to thank you on behalf of the nation, Mr Lees-Smith has contributed a great deal, more than you could possibly know." The sincerity of his condolence touched Joyce; there would be a lot of public mourning, both here and in Keighley, and then it would be her time, and then .... then she started to cry.

The emergency protocol was set in motion and a doctor, police and funeral directors arrived almost immediately. They were almost too respectful, Joyce thought, but soon they were gone, taking the body and she was left to herself. She wandered around the house, it was dark and silent. Bertie had really departed now; he loved this place, she thought, more than me in the end, but it is empty now and I shall have to leave.

She was just considering this when CJ walked through the door. He looked so good in his uniform, she was so glad Bertie had seen him rise to colonel so young. He was incredibly proud of him, although he had not always told him so, but now CJ looked like a lost boy again. Patrick was in North Africa so would not be coming home any time soon. CJ put his arms round his mother and they embraced silently.

The tributes were generous; even in the height of the war the House of Commons stopped to remember him. The funeral was attended by many more people than Joyce would have imagined possible. There were representatives from the government, the Labour party, the unions and the hospital. But Bertie had touched many people from all walks of life. John Dyer was there and heard CJ give the eulogy for his father. John found he missed Bertie but as he heard the speech, John realised the old magic had not disappeared.

Siegfried Sassoon read of Bertie's death in his comfortable inherited mansion. Leader of the Opposition, eh. You nearly made it to the top. Looking at his well manicured lawn, he could not help reflecting that he had been right when he had met Bertie after the war: neither of them had done too badly out of the manifesto. He decided to go to the wake.

The fire had gone out but logs still glowed in the fireplace. Stanley raised a glass to his old friend and looked into the dying embers; 'where are you now, my friend, you were one of a kind.'

"I didn't put you down as political," said Jimmy, Ambrose's brother, as he was talking to Muriel over a glass of restorative port. "I'm not, but he was a great fundraiser for the hospital."

"He was there from Day One."

"And a good friend," said Muriel. "We always got on well, I liked him a lot."

"Don't tell Joyce."

"She has never liked me much anyway." She turned to look at Jimmy. "And what about you – why are you here? You're not political either."

"Well Ambrose treated him latterly and...."

"And?"

"He and Joyce he always did have a wide circle of friends." He realised he had said too much.

"Tell me more," said Muriel"

"I can't – they had an understanding; anyway, neither of us will marry while our mother is still alive."

"Come on, you cannot be serious," she said, and paused. "Don't leave it too late....and you do live in such a nice house."

"It's not mine, it's not even Ambrose's."

"It may as well be," said Muriel.

She was intrigued by Jimmy. Where's that belladonna, she thought. It would be years before his mother passed on... Jimmy was right - neither of the boys did marry during her lifetime. Maybe wise, Muriel thought, Trefosa would be the mother in law from hell. Well, in the meantime Jimmy and I are both footloose and free... well, just about.

The Fox arrived. 'You certainly saved Irene, Bertie my old friend, and quite a few others it seems.' He looked round at the strong Jewish contingent led by the Rabbi of Golders Green. After the wake he invited CJ to a memorial service they were holding for his father. "We would be very honoured if you could attend."

CJ did. He was ashamed to say that although he had had several Jewish friends at school, he had never been inside a synagogue; but then, he had never been invited.

He was fascinated by the ritual; the old scrolls and candles, right here in Golders Green. Afterwards he was invited to a reception where he met Count Nikolai and some of the people who had benefited from his father's passports, including Jacob, and Olga's husband Nathaniel . Previously he had only a mere suspicion of what had happened and none at all of Patrick's role. CJ realised he had been upset when he came back from Germany but he had put it down to the bad situation in the country. He now realised that he had totally underestimated his brother; they had had the chance to talk when they had been in Suffolk together but neither of them had taken the opportunity. Anyway, the Jewish brethren were in no doubt as to who to thank for their salvation – CJ was proud to be representing the family.

By his wish, Bertie's ashes were to be scattered in Keighley. The directors of the LNER railway company were assembled at Kings Cross to meet CJ, Claire and Nigel Hawkins who escorted the ashes onto the train. Railway workers stood silently at each stop. At Leeds Nigel said a few words to the crowd. Claire was not the only one crying openly. Someone placed an engine drivers cap on the urn, where it remained. The ashes were escorted down the long platform to the small train waiting at the end. Clem Attlee led the memorial service attended by hundreds, or even more – for a moment the whole town seemed to come to a halt to say farewell; it was very moving. Some of the ashes were scattered by the War Memorial to the Pals in Oakworth Park. CJ went on his own up to Howarth, walked through the churchyard and onto the moor. It was nearly dark. It was not raining. There was a distant clap of thunder and the sky lit up briefly.

It was time to lay Bertie to rest.

On the train back to London, he fell into conversation with a girl sitting opposite, who was from the Basque country. CJ felt a strong sense of embarrassment at the British government's total failure to do anything to prevent the Spanish Civil war or ameliorate its effects. Pilar could see what he was thinking and laughed. "Please don't be embarrassed, it wasn't your fault."

"We did try to protest," he said lamely.

"Well, we are both here now and I like my new home." She

explained she had managed to get one of the last ships out of Bilbao.

"And what about you – what are you doing up here?" CJ explained. Pilar was immediately sympathetic. "I lost my brother." she said, "He died in Guernica, not in the air raid, but trying to defend it."

"I'm so sorry," said CJ.

They agreed to meet again. She kissed him lightly on the cheek.

Emma died early in the New Year. She was buried in the family crypt in Wimbledon. It was cold and dark. Joyce just felt empty.

It did not help that Bertie had not left her much money. There was very little to show for the years of service to the LSE and other university posts, let alone parliament and the government and certainly no Life Insurance policies. Percy offered to let her stay in North Square for as long as she wanted. It still did not add up and she was desperate. Count Nickolai came round one evening and she just broke down and told him the truth. He did have an idea and very soon had contacted his friends and the families of Bertie's passport holders. He raised enough cash to keep Joyce going as well as some to invest with Samuel Loebl, the rising stockbroker, who promised to do his level best for her.

 Spring arrives even in wartime and Joyce began to continue her war work with the Woman's Voluntary Service. Sadly now she had a lot in common with many other widow volunteers.

One day there was a knock on the door and the long forgotten chest arrived. Joyce managed to find the receipt and one of the men wrote 'Delivered March 1942'.

Alistair looked at the stylish Liberty's receipt and dated signature of the delivery. He felt the chest deserved its own story. No one would believe it but here was the evidence.

Joyce decided it was time to store the key parts of the family history. The chest would be perfect. So with great courage she went through the house deciding which things should be put away for posterity and what should not. New things might be added. We're not dead yet.

26 THE ARMY NAME TAG

There was a faded newspaper article: 'Another German City reaps the Whirlwind' but Patrick had not written anything about the raid in his journal. Alistair reconstructed the story from RAF records and Sarah Montagu's letter.

The senior RAF officers filed into the room at bomber command and sat round a long wooden table. Weather reports were very good, especially over Southern Germany. A list of targets was presented. The short discussion settled on Frankfurt. Further south and therefore more distant, it had not been bombed before but the RAF was getting more confident and ruthless. The meeting broke up and most of the participants went down to the canteen for tea.

One went off to ring the US Air Force to tell them of the target. "Too far south for us," came the reply. He then went to a public call box and rang the contact at the Swiss embassy. "My aunt is travelling to Frankfurt tonight." His father lived there.

In Berlin the clock was already ahead of London so it was after lunch when the intelligence came through, such as it was. "I would have picked Frankfurt myself." The Chief of Air Defence said in another meeting round another table. They all now had a grim respect for the RAF; the old adage 'the bomber will always get through' was gaining new currency as raids became increasingly lethal and the wooden heart of city after city was comprehensively destroyed by the RAF and the USAF. The men round the table knew the procedure. The pathfinder squadrons would drop markers on the main target. Before these fires could be put out there would be a heavier raid with incendiary bombs, after which came the main raid with high explosive bombs. The combined effect was usually devastating.

"I don't think they'll go for Berlin again. That leaves Frankfurt,

Wurzberg or Dresden."

"Dresden is too far for them now. There would be no American support. We have few enough planes but we could refuel and hit them hard on the way back. My bet is still Frankfurt." All round the table knew that the old city in Frankfurt was the largest in Germany. "I suppose this intelligence is credible, not some trick."

"No, it's been good in the past. Anyway, as I say, it's where I would go for. Let's do what we can."

They had one trump card to play. They sent as many mobile flack units to Frankfurt as possible. They knew from prisoners just how effective these could be and they placed them along the probable bombing runs. Another use of the intelligence was that given that they had limited number of fighters and little time to land and refuel. If they knew the target the Germans could make the grim choice of deciding whether to attack the first wave of bombers with incendiaries or the second, carrying high explosives. They contacted Frankfurt, who made their own preparations. The city authorities ordered a full evacuation of the old city and vulnerable people in other areas were also moved out. Air raid shelters were fully stocked with food and generally made ready. Local troops were moved with their anti-aircraft weapons closer to the city. Although some of the preparations could not be missed there was no general panic among the city inhabitant. Every clear night was a cause for fear as they wondered whether their city would be the next to be targeted.

One account from an RAF navigator caught his attention.

The bomber streams met over Fulda in preparation for the final run on Frankfurt just to the south.

The Lancaster lined up for the bombing run; the fires below lit up his predecessor just 200 yards ahead, inevitably at the same height and speed. The city was already well alight but the Germans were putting up tremendous fire. The next sixty seconds were the most vulnerable part of the mission. The navigator took up the controls to aim the incendiaries; he heard himself read out the distances to the target. Twenty seconds later, the near starboard engine was hit by flak. The pilot aborted straight away, diverting right and across the river. The fire caught hold and the pilot realised they would be lucky to survive. "Jettison, jettison bombs, we'll have to get back home," he said calmly.

So they dropped the incendiaries over a residential area.

The rear gunner had already been killed by a stray shot.

The fire was put out at the cost of the life of another crew member; there had been a significant loss of fuel so the pilot took the shorter emergency escape route, across France and Belgium, which also avoided the flak. The plane managed to cross the Belgium border. The gauges read zero and the crew could hear the familiar splutter of fuel-starved engines. In calm tones the navigator would never forget, the pilot told the remaining crew to jump out of the aircraft. When they were all clear he tried to crash land, avoiding any civilian areas. He was successful but hit several trees and the plane exploded before he himself had time to get out.

German radar was tracking the doomed plane and made an assessment where it had crashed and teams were dispatched to find it. Long before they arrived, friendly local ears had picked up the sound of a Lancaster in trouble and welcoming eyes had seen parachutes fall. The five remaining crewmen were rescued and spirited away to a cafe in the centre of Ypres and then down the Lifeline to Spain.

Now a major in the supply corps, Patrick found a natural flair for organisational detail during the build up to D-Day. His poor eyesight prevented him from going in on Day One – and probably saved his life, he thought. Every day after that another twenty to thirty thousand allied troops poured into Northern France, their supplies with them. As the vast armies moved westwards their supply lines got longer but if the army was to continue to function, local provisions had to be sourced and paid for with cash. The temptations were enormous. One of his sergeants was accused of misappropriation; he denied it and Patrick believed him. Patrick was overruled but he decided to fight the case. "You realise this means you will have to go back to London." So he did return and won the case.

Patrick had hitched a ride back across the Channel on the SS Forfar; there was a rudimentary lounge below and most of his fellow passengers were playing cards. Patrick was bored by this so went on deck. A sailor gave him a life jacket and insisted he wear it. He was enjoying the trip. The weather was a bit cloudy but Patrick noticed shafts of sunlight breaking through here and there. He had counted three when he noticed a different sort of shaft heading straight towards them – a torpedo. He thought he should shout a warning but he was just stunned. Others had seen it from the bridge, but there was no time to react. The torpedo hit the ship 30 yards from Patrick, with a huge explosion and the ship immediately began to list. There was a shout of 'Abandon Ship' and the crew were struggling to launch lifeboats – everybody from below was rushing on to the deck. But then the ship gave a sudden lurch and Patrick found himself flying out to sea. For a moment he seemed just suspended in mid-air. He could still see everything that was happening on the ship, as if in slow motion. Then he suddenly dropped like a stone, hitting the water – he immediately sank 10 feet. He was in total panic and shock with the cold. He could not swim but the Mae West forced him upwards and he broke the surface in the correct position to take a huge gasp of air. Luckily the water was reasonably calm so he could breathe easily without swallowing too much. His boots were dragging him down; he knew he must push them off while he still had the energy. He got one off easily but he had to bend down under water to untie the other; it did work but he was exhausted. He thought he must have lost consciousness but the water on his face woke him up. He looked round but he could not see the ship, it must have gone down. It was a lot darker now and the visibility was very limited as his head was only inches above the sea – the cold was indescribable, he knew he must keep awake. He told himself how lucky he was – lucky to have moved on to the deck, lucky that the nameless sailor had made him wear the life jacket that was saving him. He was losing consciousness regularly but then as soon as his head dropped, the icy water revived him. He thought back to his trip on the cable-laying ship; what an experience that was, with father and CJ. He had felt so close to his father, how he missed him now, but then he felt he was still with him, willing him to survive. The water revived him yet again. He realised there was a finite time that he could survive like this – he had not known he was a gambler but this was the game of his life, but he slipped into unconsciousness again and the water did not seem to revive him. Just then there was another piece of luck; a lifeboat came straight towards him. One of the crew fancied he saw a movement; they lifted him quickly out of the water with the aid of a boat hook, putting him face down on the bottom of the boat; water poured out of his lungs, causing him to cough and splutter. They slapped him on the back and more water came out but his body temperature was almost out of range. One man wrapped him in a great coat and another massaged his blue legs. A larger ship met the lifeboat and Patrick was put into a dry set of clothes and a proper bed; his temperature began to rise slowly. He woke up to see a doctor looking at him intently. "You've had a very lucky escape." He said in a Scottish accent. Patrick looked round at the unfamiliar uniforms in smart surroundings. The doctor said "You're in the Officers' Wing of the American Military Hospital in Cherbourg." The doctors soon diagnosed tuberculosis and he was flown back to London. He wrote down his experience but never spoke of it or ventured into the sea again.

He was given an honorary US Army name tag.

Alistair picked it up: LEE SMITH. The Americans never did get Lees-Smith. Stuck between the pages of Patrick's journal was a letter from a Captain Ramsay that left little to the imagination. Oh Granny, I do believe you were having a bit of fun.

27 THE SWAGGER STICK

CJ and his men crossed into Belgium. He remembered the ignominious retreat, but now the boot was literally on the other foot. They were now greeted as liberators; CJ had to brush up his French to converse with his new hosts, Flemish he never began to master. None of this mattered, the enthusiasm of the people was palpable, although CJ realised the Germans had also been somewhat popular, and significant numbers of Belgians had joined the SS.

The invasion was almost textbook, although some said that was because the Germans were managing to retreat faster than the English advanced, but they did catch the German commander of Antwerp in his bed. It was a huge prize, the most important strategic city in North West Europe. However before the port could actually be used, there was heavy fighting to free the Walcharen peninsula that bordered the river Scheldt as the Germans fought back after the Allied failure to bridge the Rhine, the bridge too far.

It was not until spring 1945 that the Rhine was crossed and they were now fighting inside Germany. The Russians were coming in from the East and the end of the war must be in sight, thought CJ.

He had been fighting for nearly six years and had managed to suspend almost everything beyond his immediate environment and survival, but now thoughts of what might happen after the war and what he might do were becoming impossible to suppress. The feeling of inadequacy had not been eliminated and his brilliant army career seemed to count for nothing; what had he really achieved? He just seemed to be contributing to the death and destruction. When his father had died he had been present for a couple of days for the funeral but then he'd had to return to his unit and get on with it, with no time to grieve. Pilar had gone to South America to look after her sick mother and the letters became fewer and fewer. Getting on with it was what the survivors in war had to do, CJ had observed. If you ever looked up at the sky, then you might well catch that stray bullet.

The Germans were still fighting hard; no rearguard actions were as effective as theirs, CJ thought. There had been some resistance in the corner of the field beyond the Rhine but the Germans had now fled and he led the battalion out of cover. Just in front of the hedge, he came across the body of a German officer, face unmarked - young and handsome, not unlike himself. It struck CJ that it could have been his bullet that had killed this man minutes before. There was a luger in the young man's hand. The bullet - and the battle – could have so easily gone the other way. He reached into the officer's breast pocket; there was a photo of his parents in a loving family group and one of a girl who stared back at him in accusation. Sister, girlfriend, wife, it did not matter. On the back of a photo there was an address in Hamburg; there seemed no point in even trying to look for his family as they had probably been wiped out in the firestorm. He gave orders to bury the body. He pocketed the photograph and took another funeral in a foreign land.

A month later they had acquired a jeep and he was being driven around in style. He was summoned to see his commanding officer back at HQ, nothing untoward, was the message. The British headquarters was in a German castle and there was an air of brisk efficiency. He was ushered in to see General Lomax. "Sit down, CJ," and he was offered some port.

"Good stuff this." There was no option with the General. "You might need it," he said, offering CJ a letter. It was from John Dyer on behalf of the Bethnal Green Labour Party offering CJ the chance to stand for parliament.

"I think the Labour party will win hands down," said the General. "They certainly will in Bethnal Green...and of course you will not be sent to Japan." He added helpfully. "All the arrangements have been made for your immediate departure. I'll say no more and leave you for a couple of minutes to think about it."

The General was as good as his word and left the room.

Even before he closed the door, CJ knew what his answer would be. This was the offer of a lifetime. He knew he would prosper in the Labour party, he had politics in the blood. Unlike Patrick, he had listened to his father's speeches from an early age – he had even served tea to Ramsay McDonald's cabinet, much to everybody's amusement – and had carried it off. He knew he had the gift of charisma and it would grow; he had the luck, even if he didn't always want it, he knew he could succeed and rise high in the party, perhaps even higher than his father.

But he also knew he had to want it, to really want it. Although he was very surprised and gratified at the offer, he was not at all as excited as he should be. He knew that if he survived the war, it had to be for a reason, but that was not politics.

When General Lomax returned, CJ thanked him and declined the offer. Pity, thought the general, I heard his father once, and CJ would be just as good, if not better.

A few days afterwards he noticed the sergeant looking perplexed, which was very unusual. "I think we had better go and see this, Sir." They drove a couple of miles through nondescript forest until they came to some barbed wire that marked the edge of some sort of camp. They continued along the perimeter and were starting to realise how big the camp must be. Through the high wire, CJ thought he noticed men in strange clothing in the distance; the jeep came to the entrance and they drove in. CJ could not believe what he was seeing. There was a pile of bodies dumped against a blockhouse like so much discarded rubbish; bodies thin and emaciated, almost merging into each other, barely human.

Further on they could see another pile and yet another. There was a command post in the middle of the camp, when they arrived, an SS officer saluted and greeted him in a friendly way – it was totally out of keeping with the surroundings. It was as if CJ was to be shown round a local health spa.

"You'd better come and see the train, Sir." Said the Sergeant.

Alistair was reading the end of Sarah Montagu's letter, whose father Solomon had been kept as a hostage by the Gestapo.

Late in the war, her brother had been killed in a car accident. Even for wartime, there seemed to be too little official concern and the investigation cursory. Although it was very hush-hush, Sarah discovered that a Swiss diplomat had been declared Persona Non Grata and forced to leave the country. Her own position seemed unaffected. Perhaps her married name had saved her. The very tenuous thread of communication with her father was severed soon afterwards. The Gestapo came round for him at 3 o'clock in the morning and he realised his luck had run out. Then began a descent into hell as he was moved from camp to camp, each one more terrible than the last, all made much worse by the numbing cold. He began to withdraw into an inner sanctum that managed to insulate his spirit from the worst of the conditions; it was beginning to warm up slightly in the spring. Eventually he ended up in a windowless railway wagon, part of a train that travelled north at night. During the day, it was parked in sidings, to avoid enemy aircraft. People were dying around him, for the most part silently as the energy to scream had long since gone.

Luckily he was in the corner of the wagon and there had been a knot that had fallen out in the timber creating a small hole; this afforded him enough space to breathe a little fresh air. His sense of time was waning, but the train had seemed to remain in this siding for a long time. Then he heard a very distant crump – he put his ear to the small hole. He had been in the German army in the First World War, it was unmistakably artillery fire; the Allies were not far away, he must conserve his remaining strength. He reached down into a pocket in his striped pyjamas and took out the last crust of bread and ate half of it.

The door slid open.

It was so bright. All he could see was the outline of a fine young Officer standing against the light, on the silhouette of a jeep. He was framed by massive gates but somehow he emanated a real sense of peace. Solomon tried to lift his arm but it did not seem to move. "This one's alive, sir." the calm voice of the Sergeant brought him back into the human race.

"Be as careful as you can, give him water but do not give him anything to eat yet - it may kill him." Gentle hands began to lift him out of the wagon. Solomon managed a scream.

The soldier said. "Leg's broken, sir."

"Use this for a splint." said the Officer handing over his swagger stick. As his eyes slowly adjusted, he could see a Union Jack on the side of the jeep – Solomon had arrived on British soil at last.

At the bottom of the chest was CJ's inscribed swagger stick.

28 THE WEDDING PHOTO

John Dyer was so proud as he surveyed Bethnal Green Town Hall. Every inch the officer, Patrick was striding up and down the tables in his smart uniform. On his arm was Norma, met while canvassing. Joyce, the veteran campaigner was rallying party workers. Not that it was required - they had waited a long time for this. Many of them had been crying openly well before the result was announced. The Labour votes piled up, dwarfing all others early in the count. The other candidates would be lucky not to lose their deposits. There was a huge clap as Percy Holman stepped forward to make his acceptance speech. It was a historic Labour landslide. Afterwards, elated, Joyce, Patrick and Norma went for a celebratory drink. Joyce was wistful for Bertie of course - this would have been his moment, but she didn't let it show.

She was watching Norma and Patrick deep in conversation; maybe, why not? Just before they left, she leant across and said to Norma casually but firmly. "Look: if you're free next Saturday please come round for tea." Norma happily accepted the invitation and did come round. On a walk with Patrick round Hampstead Heath afterwards they realised they had grown closer, and kissed.

Patrick had assumed he would take advantage of the offer of a free university place for officers but sadly was turned down on account of his TB - hence he stayed at home. His relationship with Norma deepened after more visits to Highgate. They went to a show and at a nice restaurant afterwards, Patrick proposed and was readily accepted. Soon afterwards they married. The photos captured the lovely summer's day and the great occasion brought the family back together again after the war. Norma's family were present but outnumbered. The couple honeymooned by the sea and returned to settle into their new home in Coryngham Road. Patrick did not think he had ever been so happy, he knew Norma was just right for him. He had secured a job in the new National Coal Board. He liked it and knew he could succeed, given time.

He just loved the normality now of going to work on the train and even better, coming back to Norma. There was the daily drama of rationing but that was fun for a young couple. He began to realise how much he hated the war that had so drained him and brought him close to death on several occasions. He had studiously ceased to think about his life in Germany, which he always refused to see as the enemy. Norma did know he had been there before the war but he had not told her about Anna, although she did wonder if anything had happened.

After breakfast, Ambrose was sitting in the drawing room at Uvedale looking at his beloved cabinet, his mother still had not found the drinks compartment, although he was sure she had her suspicions. His secret was safe with Elsie; although a Christadelphian, she went on regular missions to the Golders Green wine merchants to stock up. She brought in the post; there was a very official envelope, far too grand for the Inland Revenue, he thought, unless it was for a very serious transgression. Instead there was an invitation to be raised to the Peerage, become a Lord. He examined the letter and the envelope, no hoax; you could never be too careful these days, there was even the royal signature. He had to choose a title and a place – he looked up – Uvedale was the obvious choice. Place – Northend? Lord Uvedale of Northend did have a certain ring about it. Of course he was sworn to secrecy for now but he couldn't resist the temptation to tell his mother. She is so frail now but this will really please her, he thought.

He got up to look for her. She was rising increasingly late these days; there was no sign of her. He went upstairs and knocked on her door; there was no reply. He opened it, expecting some acid reproach for interfering in her privacy, but she was gone, not from the bedroom but from this world. She had died in her sleep, peacefully, as far as Ambrose could see.

She was 93 but he could still hardly believe it. He knew that without her he would probably be shining shoes in Hyde, or whatever they did there these days. She was taken back to the

Primitive Methodist chapel in Marple to be laid to rest where her husband had been Minister for so long. There was enough money to arrange a kind of chantry - a sermon to be preached every year to remember her. It still is.

Of course he and Jimmy would grieve but both knew that the end of their self-imposed bachelorhood was long overdue. There was now somebody else with whom Ambrose had to share his news.

It was a fine autumn and Patrick and Norma often walked on Hampstead Heath. There was an entrance gate not 100 yards from their front door. Then in December the weather got really cold and stayed that way. There were problems with the railways and the rest of the distribution system so coal supplies to London began to dwindle, and even worse, become a black market commodity. Other families might have ignored their principles out of necessity but Patrick worked for the National Coal Board, which was desperately trying to increase the production of coal and the delivery to where it was needed most. Edicts from London just did not work; Patrick believed in the fair distribution of resources, by rationing if necessary. If he had fought for anything during the war, it was that, so he was determined to see the crisis through. Norma became ill and there was no coal to heat the house. It was so simple - she did not want to make a fuss and Patrick went to work to help solve the national crisis. Ambrose, now Lord Uvedale, fully involved trying to keep the hospital afloat and warm, was hardly aware of the plight of Patrick's young wife. Joyce thought she was malingering, an opinion she could safely hold in the warmth of North Square. The power for the tube ran out and Patrick had to walk home. he was very late - too late. The house was very quiet. He went upstairs, Norma was still where he had left her in the morning, the large room ice cold. He tried to warm her body but it was already stiff and horribly blue. How could he have been so negligent? Why hadn't she called for help? He picked up the telephone, the line was dead.

"Death due to adverse circumstances." Said the Coroner. The cold made it difficult to dig graves but there was one already waiting for somebody else whose family had decided to delay the funeral. The vicar pressed Patrick to accept it and the next morning he went back to the church alone. "We only do graveside ceremonies these days." The vicar said, so the service was brief to non-existent. Patrick thought the vicar only came to life when he was paid the burial fee in cash. It was as if the earth had swallowed Norma up and she never had existed.

As he walked away he heard the mournful sound of a Salvation Army Band playing 'God be with you till we meet again'.

In the chest was all that was left of Norma: a brief journal, a happy wedding photo and a small envelope with the marriage and death certificates in neat copperplate handwriting. It seemed very slim. Perhaps she had been the victim of Joyce's censorship.

Of course her family never forgave him, he could hardly blame them as he could not forgive himself. This lovely creature had come into his life and he had allowed her to die. His lack of care was tantamount to murder.

He withdrew into himself, he wanted to die ... of cold as she had. He wanted to join her somewhere, wherever she was. She had gone before he had really got to know her. He dared not think of Anna.

29 THE CHIEF OF POLICE

Patrick went back to the National Coal Board and tried to bury his grief in work but his will to live was sapped as the shadow on the lung returned. It was just beginning to warm up in April when he felt unwell again; he knew what it was. If in any way he was recovering from his loss, it all came back to him now. This time Ambrose took personal charge. The TB had progressed and even with all his skill, Ambrose had no choice but to cut deep and leave Patrick with only three quarters of a lung. There would be a long recuperation in the Manor House Hospital under the care of Sister Mcglashan. Ambrose only knew the boys fleetingly through Joyce and his relationship with her was, well...unofficial. Superficially both were now fine young officers who had taken their father's death in their stride and were in no hurry for any kind of replacement, even if that was on the cards. While Ambrose had plenty of experience of being a son, albeit downtrodden, he had none of being a father. He realised that both Bertie and Joyce had been far too busy to be there for the boys. He had hardly met CJ at all and he had been the closest to his mother anyway. Gradually over the months Ambrose took time to listen to Patrick. Initially he apologised for failing to do more to look after Norma. He felt her death could have been avoided if only Joyce had not always been so insistent Norma had been malingering. However Ambrose slowly began to uncover some of the traumatic experiences over the six years of warfare; shooting the dog at Dunkirk; the desperate cries of the doomed Spitfire pilot; fighting unconsciousness in the face of numbing cold of the Channel. Instinctively suspicious of the Officer class, Ambrose developed a new respect for Patrick and he for Ambrose. Lily was a frequent visitor. Between them they got Patrick to talk more about Frankfurt before the war and it's devastation by the RAF. He had no idea what happened to Anna.

Patrick was well enough to be moved to the General Ward. He found himself next to Andrew Stewart, a miner from Glasgow with emphysema. They became very good friends as they whiled away the long hours lying in bed with stories. Andrew had been wounded in the First World War and had woken up on a railway platform in France. Bodies were laid side by side as far as he could see. There was a large 'E' pinned to his chest and a 'G' on the unconscious man laid next to him. Hoping to get back to Glasgow rather than Edinburgh, he swapped the labels round before slipping back into unconsciousness.

"My father was a stretcher bearer and the story of the labels was a bit of a legend. I did not realise it was true," said Patrick.

Of course the labels had been nothing to do with destination. Nevertheless some time later, Andrew arrived in a siding at Stobhill, the huge casualty hospital outside Glasgow. Each ward seemed liked a small hospital and there were 50 of them spread over square miles. Andrew was fortunate in his last stop. His doctor was the experienced Wishart Kerr who had spent many years as a medical missionary and was now in general practice in Cambuslang, Glasgow, volunteering for Stobhill. The doctor rapidly diagnosed the problem was Andrew's eye and was audibly cursing whoever had made the original assessment. "It was me, doctor. I swapped the sign on my chest," came a voice. It was impossible to be annoyed with this big-hearted man for long. "Well, you've arrived at the right place." The doctor replied, recognising the Glasgow twang. "No more tricks. I'm on your case now".

"Thanks, Doctor."

"Kerr, Wishart Kerr. You've been lucky to get here. We'll be looking after you now." He said reassuringly as he turned towards the next bed.

"O Doctor, you couldn't tell my sisters I'm here, could you"

"Where do they live?"

"They run a pharmacy in Bridgeton."

"It's on my way home. I'll call."

"That would be ever so kind, Doctor." His tone touched Wishart.

He found the pharmacy in Bridgeton easily and walked in. He was caught in the sharp gaze of a striking young woman with large blue eyes. He was stunned, she held his gaze for a long time, he felt like a teenager, all his varied past life just disappeared.

"Dr Kerr." She said softly after a while. "I'm Barbara Stewart – I remember you gave a first aid talk to the local ambulance drivers. How can I help you?"

"It's your brother Andrew, I'm treating him at Stobhill." He managed to blurt out.

"Is he all right?"

He could not tell a lie; "I'm afraid I think he will lose the sight of his right eye."

Barbara was shocked but very strong. "I'm sure you are trying your best." She said, picking up his obvious concern.

"When can we visit him?"

"Oh any time. I can take you there now if you like." Hearing himself go way beyond the call of duty.

"My sisters and I will certainly accept your offer. On condition that you will come round to tea. You and your family."

"Oh, I'm a widower. But I'd love to come. When Andrew is better, of course. He's a remarkable young man."

After time romance blossomed; they got married and Barbara became pregnant. Wishart drove her to hospital for the birth. Despite a doctor's Red Cross on the car, it was stoned on the way as Wishart had to navigate through a riot during the General Strike.

Ambrose happened to be passing and told them he had seen the whole thing.

May, their daughter, had a happy childhood with blissful holidays going up the Clyde to Arran on the 'The Pride of Brodick'.

"That's the ship that rescued me from Dunkirk. The crew were incredibly brave." Patrick said and he began to tell Andrew about his war experiences.

The traumatic circumstances surrounding her birth seemed to rub off on May, who became a lifelong Conservative supporter. Although still a student at Glasgow University, she had been the party agent in an unwinnable seat on Red Clydeside in 1945. The son of a Lord, the candidate's sole purpose was to avoid being sent out to the Far East to fight. When Japan surrendered, his small interest in proceedings shrunk visibly, though he was still forced to go to public meetings. He was challenged to live on a pound a week, the current level of welfare payment. He did manage, spending a third of his money on postage stamps, but it transpired his friends had taken him out to dinner each night. He lost his deposit.

"I met Norma at the election." Patrick said and Andrew listened.

Ambrose had a thought. He and Joyce went to Count Nickolai and explained the situation. He thought for a moment. "Look, I still have contacts over here. Patrick is nearly recovered now. Let me arrange a holiday, not to Frankfurt itself – what's left of it – to Triburg in the Black Forest, and then to Heidelburg. I can arrange a cash pick up in Frankfurt. He can then explore further if he wishes; otherwise it's a health cure. Agreed? ...Oh, don't worry. Everything will be paid for. That is the least we can do."

Patrick began to feel there might be another life. Then he had an unexpected visitor. Other than as an acquaintance of his father, he hardly knew Count Nickolai or anything about him. However the Count seemed to know a lot more about Patrick.

"We have never thanked you for your actions." He was saying.

"What on earth are you talking about?" Patrick asked.

"Delivering the parcel to the Church."

"I never knew what the fuss was about, although I was thrown out on my ear."

"I know and I am sorry - I owe you an explanation. " So he told Patrick about the passports.

"I see." Said Patrick slowly. He had a thousand questions but he knew most of them could never be answered now. They were two wives away; he had always considered Anna and he had been married in the Stadtwald. "I suppose I must thank you for telling me. "

"And we will be forever in your debt. Forty families are here now that otherwise would not have survived. I have talked with your mother and Ambrose. You can take a holiday in the Black Forest. It is all arranged. No foreign exchange limits. I still have people over there who will provide you with marks. These are the pickup points. All the accommodation is paid for. What do you say?" Patrick looked through the itinerary: Two weeks in Triburg and then a couple of days in Heidelburg. He could not believe it.

"I'm speechless. I'm glad I helped although I had no idea what with until now."

"You leave tomorrow, before you change your mind."

Patrick packed his bag and said goodbye to Andrew. He said. "If you wait a moment, May will be along. She is in London for a meeting. You two would get along so well. "

"I'm afraid I've got to catch the boat train." Patrick replied. There was a revolving door on the way out and as he was going through, Patrick noticed the smart young woman on the other side of the door. There was a grouse claw on her jacket. His foot paused but then continued towards the waiting taxi.

Patrick reached Triburg and stepped back into a world that harked back to the Middle Ages. The Black Forest was as beautiful as ever and young men still walked round in lederhosen.

He left for Heidelburg and found the small gasthof that Nickolai had booked. The landlady was a young widow called Gertrude. Patrick did not pry. She thought Patrick looked very sad underneath the surface. He was the only guest. She showed him the room. But when he realised she would have to sleep on the sofa downstairs, he insisted she have the room.

Patrick took the train to Frankfurt Hauptbahnhof to get some more marks from the address he had been given. The station no longer existed. He got off at the only remaining platform. It was all wasteland; the beautiful old town now charred ruins. He just recognised Rose Corner and the Freyhof fountain, where he and met Anna so many times. The raid had taken place on the 112th anniversary of Goethe's death but now his birthplace had been destroyed too. He continued to walk round the ruins of the old town and then took a ferry across the river as all the bridges were down. There was less damage as he walked away from the Old Town. He could not resist going to see Anna's house. The trams and buses seemed just as efficient as before the war, except over the bridges. He got off at Anna's stop. Although he had told himself this trip would not be a good idea, he walked up the street with rising excitement as feelings long-suppressed began to rise to the surface. He turned the corner and saw the rubble that had been the house. He turned and ran, not wanting to see or think any more. He got himself together with several schnapps in a bar and became almost maniacally confident.

He went to the central Police Station. Reinhart Schmidt was now Frankfurt Chief of Police. He greeted Patrick with surprising friendliness and took him to a Bierkeller like an old friend. "It is time to get drunk," he said, buying Patrick a schnapps and making him down it. He then told Patrick what had happened.

During the big raid, a bomber had been hit, strayed across the river and jettisoned its incendiary bombs over a residential district, most fell harmlessly but one lodged in the roof of the Schmidt's house. It burned silently. Dinka, the servant living in the outhouse woke up with the smell of burning. She rushed into the courtyard and tried raise the family. She managed to break Anna's upstairs window with a stone but it was too late. There was an explosion and Gunter, Gerda and Anna were all killed. Nothing was left of the house. He paused to let Patrick digest this and went off to get a couple of large steins. Patrick was staring into space. There was nothing for it but to plough on.

Reinhart continued gently. "Anna had a son Eric, but perhaps you already knew that." Patrick shook his head slowly." "He was yours. Eric died as well, killed by the RAF. "

 Patrick was reminded by Reinhard of his last trip to the Hauptbahnhof. He could not help but notice Anna's strong feelings for Patrick and had realised then she was pregnant. Reinhard had confronted her while Patrick was getting his things from the flat. She admitted it and said she loved him. Patrick had come back quickly and they had continued to the station.

Not the greatest family man, he had always liked his niece and he felt really sorry for her now. Her brother had then been an arrogant little shit. They reached the station and Reinhard had taken Anna a couple of tables away and said. "Look. It's not my business. It will never work, wherever you both are. You'll have to end it. He won't. But if you can't..." Anna was just staring at him. "I will buy two tickets to Basle." "No, I couldn't.....He doesn't know." She said, almost to herself. "And he mustn't. Not yet."

Reinhard let Patrick stare into his beer. At last he almost whispered. "Did you find her body? "

"No." Said Reinhard. "Nor Eric's. Believe me we tried. We found my brother and Greta."

"And Lothar?" asked Patrick.

"I know you two did not get on too well but he was beginning to grow out of the Hitler Youth. He was killed in Russia three weeks after the start of the invasion. He was in the Panzers."

Patrick nodded. "I saw him… briefly." and he told Reinhard about the fleeting glimpse at Dunkirk.

"Anyway in the last letter he wrote was this picture of thousands of tanks stretching across the Russian steppes, taken just before Lothar's group headed towards the Baltic States. I'm surprised it got through the censors. Then nothing. The family were getting worried; despite the huge propaganda and hype, rumours were beginning to abound that all was not going well with the grand attack on Russia and of new deadly enemy tanks. A short time later there was a knock on their door and two elderly army officers told them that Lothar had died bravely leading his men for the Fatherland. No, his body would not be coming home. He had been buried with full military honours in Russia. Nine months later his sergeant, Gert, had come to tell the family what had happened. He was a nice bloke. Made a pass at Anna." Patrick reacted angrily.

"O nothing happened." Lothar actually died in Estonia. Buried in a churchyard next to the commander of the Russian tank that killed him."

"I'm sorry," said Patrick.

Reinhart continued. "There is a family grave in the Lutheran Church of Saint John." They sat in silence.

Eventually Patrick said. "That was where I left those passports. I only recently found out what was in the package."

"At the time, I could see you had no idea what you were doing." Reinhard replied. " Well you certainly did them all a big favour. It was only later in the war I had any idea what might actually be happening to all the Jews I was rounding up." He paused. "Strangely enough it was Anna who told me. She knew someone who worked in one of the camps. As Lothar became more reasonable, she went the other way, especially after he had been killed. ....I'm sorry to say it was almost fortunate she was killed. She would be a War Criminal now. It's completely changed now, almost shoot on sight... Terrible things were done by both sides."

"Just what did Anna do, or was supposed to have done?" asked Patrick. "Oh, nothing to do with the camps. She was in an Army unit that was responsible for Art work. Well, that was the official version back then. I think she was a courier taking stolen pictures into Switzerland."

"Is that a War Crime?"

"It is if some of them came from the Amber Room in the Czar's Palace in St Petersburg. Our Russian masters take that very seriously, as do the Western Allies. They should never have been taken, of course."

"She was always interested in pictures. They became her downfall it seems." Said Patrick philosophically.

Reinhard sat back and looked at Patrick. Actually he had always liked him, never more so than now. They both needed to talk and not to be alone tonight. Reinhard continued. "Lothar had a girl, Piret. Greta went to see her in Estonia. She had only just got back before the raid." Reinhart paused. Patrick could see he was beginning to get upset, but he had to continue the story. "They met at a Liberation celebration the night before he died. She and Lothar had a daughter, also Greta." "What happened to them?" asked Patrick.

"I am now in a position to make enquiries. Gert married her to make sure she and Greta could get out of Estonia. They were evacuated to Koenigsberg (now Kaliningrad)." Reinhart went off to buy two more steins. He continued. "The story begins to get hazy now. The city was beginning to fill up with refugees and I think she wanted to reach here. "

"Frankfurt?"

"Yes, and here's the thing. I was interviewing the commander of a Tiger tank and he told me a story…

His lone Tiger tank stood on the east side of the last Oder bridge still standing. Two Russian T34s were watching him just 50 yards away; both sides could see each other clearly but the German realised that even if he destroyed one tank he would have to turn round to cross the bridge and the other tank would be able to hit his exposed rear and knock him out. The Russians realised that if they did destroy him on this side of the bridge, it would be blown up as soon as they began to cross it. The political commissar was nowhere near the front line, he had probably found a woman, the tank commander was thinking, so there was no need for heroics now. In the brief standoff a young woman and her small child ran out between the tanks towards the Tiger. The Russian tank commander put up his hand; the German acknowledged him and let the woman cling on while he managed to put the child into the tank. He saluted the Russians, turned his tank round and rumbled over the bridge. When they had crossed safely, the bridge was blown up and fell spectacularly into the river. Piret and Greta had reached Frankfurt, but it was Frankfurt on Oder.

"Maybe she had just picked the wrong Frankfurt." Said Patrick.

"Perhaps. Now it's in the Soviet zone. But I like to think she was coming here. That is as far as I have got." concluded Reinhard. "Oh, and Gert was captured and sent to Siberia. I think he is still there."

They had another schnapps but it did not remove the chill.

"And what happened to your own family?" Asked Patrick.

Reinhart grimaced. "They all survived and are in rude health. We no longer sing 'Tomorrow belongs to me' at dinner. None of them were ever good singers anyway."

"Where is Dinka now?" Asked Patrick. "I think she moved to her sister Helga's in Heidelburg."

Patrick was very unsteady on his feet as he made his way to the Hauptbahnhof, or what was left of it. It was dark and he thought he saw someone following him in the shadows but supposed it was the drink. The cafe where he had said goodbye to Anna was still there and he got himself a cup of coffee and stared out of the window. He looked up and there really was a ghost in the reflection. A familiar voice said. "You've lost weight and your suit is too big for you. Otherwise you don't look bad at all."

30 DICK WHITTINGTON

Patrick and Anna just held each other for a long while before a waitress pointedly asked Patrick if he wished to order. He apologised and they went out into the night air. He did not press but assumed that she would get round to tell him about Eric. He listened as she described what happened in the air raid. She was woken by a stone breaking her bedroom window. The house was well alight. She grabbed Eric..." She stopped.

"Reinhard told me about him." Patrick said.

"I should have told you, I'm sorry."

"No, I should have stayed and faced the consequences."

"Then neither of us would be still here."

"So what happened then?"

"I managed to open the window and throw Eric down to Dinka, who just caught him. I tried to rescue mum and dad but the heat was intense. There was an explosion and I was thrown clear of the house. I woke up much later amongst shrubs in the garden, I was only slightly bruised. The house had burnt to the ground and there was no one about. I considered my options. I knew the war was lost. The Russians would not easily forgive what I had done. I would never see Eric again."

"Where is Eric?" Said Patrick, sensing all was not right.

"I just assumed that I would meet up with Dinka and take Eric back. But I presume she thought he would go to Reinhard and that would be the end of it. She did not like Reinhard, or his wife. I had no idea she would take it on herself to spirit him away."

"You had no option. You saved his life. Reinhard said she had gone to live with her sister in Heidelburg."

"She may well have done but I could not find either of them...and believe me I have looked." Patrick could see she was on the edge of tears.

"Look – of course we have to find him. But you must keep a low profile. We must be careful, even when we meet. Please tell me what happened to you."

"I got war work easily enough and a new identity and I melted into the underclass. After the war, things got, if anything, worse. The underclass was swelling with war criminals on the run, refugees with no papers, Russians and others who had fought for Germany who faced a poor future back east. We are all looking for a way out of the 'Twilight Zone'. "

"Look, I will search for Eric." Despite her protests, he gave her a wad of marks. They kissed and agreed to meet again in the reasonably anonymous station bar. A plan was beginning to form in Patrick's mind.

Meanwhile Lord Uvedale was getting into his stride. One of the new government promises was to create a comprehensive free health service. Ambrose was instinctively suspicious of government interference in medicine, preferring the subscription approach of the Manor House Hospital. He was not alone in the Labour Party. However, the government were looking for sympathetic external nominees for a new committee to draw up proposals and advise the Health Minister, Aneurin Bevan. This might suit Joyce very well.

When she received the job offer, Ambrose did not look entirely surprised. "This is your doing, I suppose – I'll fight my own battles if you don't mind. But I suppose I'll go along just to see what it's like."

She took to the new work like a duck to water. Her journal described the position: the current health provision was a huge patchwork, the prestigious London teaching hospitals stood at one end, some of which had international reputations. At the other end were as many as 90,000 Poor law beds, many of which would not look out of place in the poorest parts of the world, ghosts of the workhouse, little better than living morgues. Between them was the large voluntary sector, again very variable in quality. Bang in the middle was the Manor House hospital. Joyce could see the vision of joining them together as a coherent whole. And then there were the doctors …

It would have been a huge achievement just to overcome all the vested interests and put all the hospitals into one organisation but Aneurin and the Committee saw that it would never work without the doctors, represented by the BMA, unwaveringly opposed to being directly employed by the State. They could teach us a thing or two about trade union negotiation, Aneurin thought.

He agreed that joining the new system could only be achieved if there was a majority in a secret ballot among the doctors. The BMA walked out, confident that their members would never vote for it.

Aneurin and the Committee did have a trick or two up their sleeves; the tens of thousands of doctors who had just served in the armed forces were nowhere near as hostile to the new health service concept as the BMA would have you think. If the leading surgeons could also be persuaded to join, the BMA would be isolated.

The Royal College of Surgeons was an ancient body which had few members and the arcane public voting procedure of publicly putting a pebble in a large dish, so every individual vote would count. In an epic alliance of mutual self- interest, Aneurin found an unusual partner in patrician Lord Moran, the arch establishment figure and offered him unlimited money and control over the hospitals. Then came the rounds of individual persuasion and arm-twisting.

The minister was seeing Ambrose in his office. "I would have thought you would be in favour of this." Aneurin said.

"The members want the security of their subscriptions." Ambrose replied. "But they would be treated locally and referred to you if necessary. You're not trying to blackmail me are you, Ambrose? Will I have to stuff your mouth with gold?"

"A little would be nice."

"I need your surgeon's vote so I will listen to your objections when the time comes. I do have a spy in your camp though."

"We are not joined at the hip, not just yet anyway."

"I thought you specialised in knees!" Aneurin retorted.

Aneurin won the battle and the BMA were forced to concede to the new system, albeit with contractor status. The NHS was born and Joyce became the first chairperson of the new North West London Hospital Board. She set up her headquarters in the Dick Whittington Hospital in Bethnal Green. If this works here, she thought, it will work anywhere. A young gynaecologist moved into an office along her corridor. He had an engaging smile and introduced himself as Patrick Steptoe. "I've a son named Patrick." said Joyce.

"I hope I live up to him." Dr Steptoe replied.

"You'll be fine." Joyce said. If they are all like that, she thought, we will not go far wrong.

Joyce's financial health was also improving. Samuel Loebl had been as good as his word and Joyce's initial capital was growing considerably.

She was also invited to become a JP in Hendon. She walked into the courtroom. Everyone rose and clapped. She acknowledged it. 'I can still hold a crowd', she thought as she sat on the bench with two other JPs. In the next room a policeman looked at an unlucky burglar caught in the act. "There's a new woman magistrate today. They're the worst, trying to prove they can punish. You're in for a nasty shock, my old son." The burglar quailed visibly.

"Perks, why are you back here? You know what this means."

"I've a young son to feed now, m'lady."

Joyce looked at the young man. He motioned to the gallery where there was a young girl with a baby.

She looked at her colleagues. They nodded. "Oh all right, £10. But this is the last time." She said firmly but kindly. "At ten shillings a week."

Perks looked horrified and opened his mouth to protest.

"Five." said Joyce. "And I do not want to see you here again."

"Thank you, m'lady."

The policeman smiled. It was the right punishment.

"I find trying to run one hospital hard enough, how on earth do you manage with 10?"

"Cash - if you control the purse strings the stethoscopes and scalpels usually follow."

"I can imagine that, be careful with the scalpels though." said Ambrose.

"You'd better watch out, I'm going to be taking over your hospital lock, stock and barrel so I'll expect a bit more respect."

"We'll have to see about that."

"Do you seriously think the Manor House will escape?" asked Joyce.

Ambrose showed her the Letters Patent and other regalia that came with being a Lord. She had to admit she was impressed.

In the chest was all the regalia fit for Lord Uvedale.

After the war CJ stayed on in Germany as part of the occupying forces and participated in the reconstruction. He went to a conference in Trier on joint Iron and Steel production. He fell in with a diplomat from Luxembourg called Jean Paul. As usual there was no agreement, so the conference ended a day early. Jean Paul said to CJ. "Look, we have accommodation here, you are not expected back in Cleves and I not in Luxembourg, I hate to think what I might find if I came back a day early!"

"I'm sorry."

"Don't be; let me show you a nice place in Germany – how do you say - we may as well be hung for a sheep as for a lamb." So they went to Heidelburg. There was bomb damage all around. They were on the bridge taking in the view of the ruined castle - why did that look so different? They walked on and found the splendid undamaged baroque St Pauls Kirche on Baseler Strasse. CJ loved the gilded carving and the alterpiece looked very like a Rubens.

Later, as they drank coffee in the cafe next door, they struck up a conversation with a young woman, she introduced herself as Dinka.

"I am about to pick up my son Eric from school, can I show you a little more of Heidelburg?"

They all walked to Eric's school together and waited for him. Dinka told them she had worked in a well-to-do house in Frankfurt before the war and a little about the terrible raid. Christopher found her matter-of-fact account very upsetting. She explained she was now living with her son in the house of Helga, her widowed sister. Eric came out, a fine young boy who readily smiled at Jean Paul and CJ. He looked strangely familiar but CJ did not think about it further. They gratefully accepted an invitation to supper with Dinka and her sister in their small flat. Jean Paul provided a bottle of wine and the evening went very smoothly. Eric loved talking to them and trying to speak French and English. Dinka seemed very interested in CJ's brother, especially when CJ said he was very concerned about Patrick, now ill with TB.

Jean Paul and CJ both insisted that the sisters come out for a drink, and they accepted gratefully. They left Eric with a neighbour and walked round to the bierkeller. There was no traditional dress and dancing on the table but the beer was good.

The conversation flowed even more easily and Dinka asked again about Patrick and the fact he'd married after the war. CJ paused – he knew he shouldn't go on but the schnapps was very warming. "But she died of cold."

There was silence.... Jean Paul said quietly and with genuine concern. "Here you are over here trying to organise our Iron and Steel production while your own citizens are dying of cold."

"You have no idea," said CJ. "Our rations are less than yours."

"You're right, we really do not have any idea, you really did sacrifice a lot to win the war, but if you only realise, it's yours to win the peace. We need you here in Europe but you will need us too. I really hope you will solve your problems; we will get iron and steel running again but afterwards we could all be so much better together. It's so obvious from where I live in Luxembourg – all our neighbours have invaded us, Germany most recently, and conscripted all our young men, like it or not. My own son was killed in Russia but he will not have died in vain if in 50 or 70 years time we are all still together in Europe."

They drank some more and the conversation lightened again. At the end, Jean Paul and Dinka got up and went off to discuss steel production, leaving Helga and CJ talking, enjoying the atmosphere. At length he looked across at her. "I've really enjoyed the evening. I appreciate your kindness and hospitality," he said. "I hope when Patrick was here, he met people like you." She looked very moved.

They got up and walked slowly towards the station. She turned and kissed him on the cheek. "You need somebody too ......or something." He shook her hand and gave her his card. She waved him goodbye.

A couple of months later, when CJ was demobbed he took up the offer of a free university place. He got off the train at Oxford and was assaulted by the smell of horseradish from the factory opposite the station. He hurried past Halls Brewery, smelling of hops. Not quite the introduction to academia I had hoped, he thought. He walked over the bridge and disappeared into the colleges.

He was early for his interview so he walked along the High and stopped at The Mitre for a cup of tea. It was served on a silver tray. I could get used to this, he thought. He was beginning to feel on the right path at last. He mused over his time in Germany and that last visit to Heidelburg. It had been so nice meeting the sisters and Eric, such a nice boy. And such a lovely church; for once Patrick had been so interested. *There was a print of the magnificent Rubens altarpiece.*

31 SANCTUARY

It was Muriel who actually proposed, deciding that she would probably be dead before Jimmy got round to it. She insisted on a new start, living at her home and making Jimmy leave the cocoon of Uvedale. However they did have their reception there and the house did them proud.

Joyce was drowning her sorrows. Ambrose came across. "Are you enjoying it?" he asked.

"No." She replied bluntly. He could see she was very upset – he knew she had always been jealous of Muriel but this went much deeper, her vulnerability very apparent. "You only have to ask you know." He said gently.

She faced him. "No, it's you who have to ask," she said. She looked so attractive and luckily tears had not spoilt her makeup.

"Joyce, I am asking you to be my wife – I love you, I have always loved you."

"I can't say no to that, my Lord, I will accept." Joyce had to admit that becoming a Lady helped and who would not like to live in Uvedale?

But they had known each other for a lot longer than any of that.

Joyce was determined to put on a good show. She persuaded Ambrose to move up from the Mission Hall, sincere though that might be, to the Savoy Chapel. Uvedale was not quite Berkeley Square or Wallington but it did have something of its own and now it would be getting a new mistress. The surviving Holmans would be there, of course, and Percy, now rather grand in his own right, would be giving her away - her sons , Patrick looking rather good in his new suit, and CJ, who had always looked better in uniform, and on Ambrose's side, Jimmy with Muriel.

Joyce heard the familiar words being intoned and could not help remembering the first time – she had been so young, her mother had been right about that; she didn't regret it though, they'd had a life. She'd made mistakes, of course, but not important ones, she felt. She had loved Bertie in her own way, and he had loved her too; something had been held back towards the end, on both sides. It had probably suited them both and it had not prevented a long marriage - now she was embarking on another adventure. She and Ambrose retired into the vestry to sign the register. They heard the piano playing and Muriel started to sing. 'Falling in love again'. Yes, thought Joyce, that's what I'm doing and she came back into the church as Lady Uvedale.

She thanked Percy for giving her away; they both wished Emma had been here to see the wedding. "And now I suppose you're going to evict me from North Square," she said mischievously.

"Funny you should say that," replied Percy. "I'm not a totally unfeeling landlord. I've had a word with the Manor House Hospital and they are prepared to let you live in Uvedale if you perform certain duties."

"Well, I won't be emptying bedpans, if that's what you think!"

"Perhaps they might find you something else." Percy smiled.

Joyce remembered how they had come upon the site of the Hospital over 30 years ago. Who would dream she would be living in Uvedale now?

 CJ was talking to John Dyer. "I want to thank you for the invitation to become your MP. My heart just wasn't in it and that would not have been fair to you, the party or the constituents. Anyway you got Uncle Percy instead."

"What are you going to do?" Asked John.

"Oh, I am studying theology. I want to join the church."

"Good Luck. Our loss is very much their gain," said John and they shook hands.

Patrick could not help telling Lily about Frankfurt., and what happened to Anna. Lothar had stayed at Beech Court and he told her all about him too. She sensed there was more. She took him outside and he told her about Eric.

He was also awaiting the result of another TB test which might mean he would have to go to Switzerland to convalesce.

Charles and Mary Trevelyan couldn't make it but sent along their butler to prepare Uvedale for the reception and act as an MC.

The wedding party set off for Uvedale and were met by a cheering crowd of staff. On the steps was Sister Mcglashan, who had been there from the beginning. The crowd was silent as Aneurin Bevan moved forward and presented Ambrose with a large Frank Salisbury portrait, the wedding present from the hospital staff. He raised his hand and said.

"Ambrose Woodall is a great surgeon, who over the last thirty years, with your help, has transformed a motley group of temporary wartime buildings into the reality of the fine modern Trade Union Hospital we are in today. I have decided to let the Manor House continue on it's own path and leave it out of the new National Health Service." The crowd cheered again. Ernie Bevin was also present and gave Ambrose a large wink.

The painting now hung above the Coronation chairs in Alistair's hall.

In the evening Joyce and Ambrose held their first ball. Lily accepted a glass of champagne and looked round the room. There was Ethel and John Dyer, who had rescued Bertie all those years ago; Siegfried Sassoon who had made his name; Nigel and Claire Hawkins who had secured his political base. I think Bertie would have given his blessing, she thought. She looked at Joyce, now very much the lady of the house entertaining Ambrose's eminent medical colleagues and new political friends from the House of Lords.

Across the room, Solomon Lewin thanked CJ for rescuing him and handed back the swagger stick. "This belongs to you."

"Well, we did get you back to Britain in the end," said CJ. Lily noticed Patrick talking earnestly to Count Nickolai. Sarah Montague was with them. She handed Patrick something that looked very much like a new passport. The Count passed him a piece of paper with codes across the top. There was a man with them who could only be described as anonymous. Was the Fox helping to plan some more private enterprise? Patrick's not at school any more, she thought, and I'm not a headmistress. Good Luck to him! Elsie brought her another glass of champagne. "A change for you," said Lily.

"His Lordship is so happy," was all she would say, smiling. The sparkle bought to mind Berkeley Square. Now Joyce really was having her own ball … and a grandson, did she but know it.

The music struck up – Bridget, hiding behind a pillar, mesmerised by the spectacle. You're way beyond Beech Court now, Lily thought. She watched Joyce and Ambrose lead the dancing, so elegant. Perhaps she's beyond worrying about her children, anyway, I'm no longer the chaperone.

The House embarked on the golden era for which it had been so well designed.

Reinhard had not been quite fair about his own family; One of his sons, another Gunter, was a rising start in the new German Diplomatic Corps and was Charge d'Affaires in London. Ernie Bevin, now Foreign Secretary, had asked Gunter to come along to the ball at Uvedale. "I remember Patrick from Frankfurt before the war." He was saying. "I heard he had to leave early."

"Probably homesick," said Ernie quickly.

In the chest was a silver picture frame inscribed to Sister Mcglashan on her retirement and in it a photo of her receiving a gift and a large bouquet of flowers from Ambrose. Sandy, the security guard would really appreciate that, thought Alistair. And he presented it to him, along with a fine wedding photo of Joyce and Ambrose.

Had the chest been walled up deliberately or just forgotten?

Joyce had just remarried and wanted to make a fresh start - Ambrose might even have demanded it.

It did not quite ring true. The chest had not yet yielded up all it's surprises.

Alistair picked up a large manila envelope laying on the bottom of the chest, He opened it. There was a long letter in German but it had a typewritten translation.

It was from Helga who had got the address of Uvedale from CJ.

On the night of the Frankfurt raid, Dinka had managed to break the window of Anna's first floor bedroom with a stone, waking her. Dinka could just make out her expression of terror but she managed to open the window and throw Eric down to Dinka, who just caught him. But that was the last she saw of Anna. Soon afterwards there was an explosion and the house went up in flames.

In the aftermath of the raid the attention of the authorities was on the centre of the city which had been totally devastated. There had been no firestorm and the evacuation of the city had drastically reduced the number of casualties to thousands rather than tens of thousands. The authorities assumed Eric had perished along with the rest of his family. Dinka loved Eric and somehow could not bring herself to give him up. His uncle, the policeman, should be the one to look after him. She did not like him and also knew his reputation - Eric would be better off with her. A few days later she went to the joint funerals of the family, she did not bring Eric and she did not feel guilty. She moved with Eric to her sister in Heidelburg.

They all survived the war and Eric grew up a fine boy. Then suddenly Jean Paul and CJ arrived out of the blue. It was obvious that he was the brother of Patrick. In the evening, after the sisters found out what had happened to him, there had been a lull in the conversation and they had excused themselves. "You must tell him, it's only right." Said Helga. "He's a widower, what can he do? He should never have left Anna in the first place. "Replied Dinka.

"You never liked him. He would be dead by now if he had stayed. Eric could be just what he needs."

"He's not well, he's had TB," said Dinka in a hardening tone. Helga felt if only she had taken the job in Frankfurt herself instead of giving it to her sister. CJ had looked so pensive and had such a mesmerising voice, she could have just told him everything there and then, he had so nearly guessed the truth. But he had given Helga his name and address.

Now Eric had been kidnapped. A young woman in dark glasses who said she was Eric's aunt had walked into the school. Eric had shown some recognition and had walked off with her across the playground and into a smart Mercedes, driven by a young man also in dark glasses. As Dinka crossed the road to pick up Eric, she noticed the man get out of a Mercedes to fill up with petrol. As he bent down there was something familiar about him that she could not place. The car travelled south. There was a police report of a Mercedes with two passengers speeding down the autobahn to Basle and the Swiss Border. At the time there was no reason to stop the car other than speed. Anyway the Mercedes would be hard to catch, especially if well driven. And there was a true professional behind the wheel according to the report.

Alistair put down the letter from Germany. Behind the story was a plea for help. Eric was Joyce's first grandchild. There was a train ticket from Frankfurt. Might she have gone to meet the sisters and try to find Eric? There was a fragment of a letter from Patrick. Did she think he was involved? Had it been ripped up in anger?

When Bertie had died in 1941, he could not have known just how valuable the passports would be to their recipients but the Lees-Smith's had paid a price.

But there was one last surprise. Before Alistair closed the chest he noticed an old RSPB magazine with the avocet on the front cover. He opened it to a picture of CJ and Patrick in uniform poring over a map; two young officers taking an important decision.

After the war they tried to reinstate the dykes but to no avail. So the birds have continued to stay over at what has become the premier bird sanctuary at Minsmere. The avocet prospered and continues to symbolise the RSPB.

Alistair opened the window wide. The heron flew off into the sunset.

The chest came into my possession some years ago. I have been fascinated by its origins since, as a small child my grandmother regaled me with its story. On retirement I began researching my family history, particularly that of Bertie, my grandfather, of whom I am very proud. I thought of combining the two stories - this is the result.

Printed in Poland
by Amazon Fulfillment
Poland Sp. z o.o., Wrocław